Date Due

DEC 2 '04			
DEC 16 '04			
FEB 7 2008			

BRODART, INC. Cat. No. 23 233 Printed in U.S.A.

DISCARD

the beckoners

the beckoners

carrie mac

ORCA BOOK PUBLISHERS

National Library of Canada Cataloguing in Publication Data

Mac, Carrie, 1975-
The beckoners / Carrie Mac.

ISBN 1-55143-309-5

I. Title.

PS8625.C3B43 2004 jC813'.6 C2004-903706-4

Library of Congress Control Number: 2004108679

Summary: When Zoe moves to a new town, she finds the line between victim and tormentor is easily crossed.

Orca Book Publishers gratefully acknowledges the support for its publishing programs provided by the following agencies: the Government of Canada through the Book Publishing Industry Development Program (BPIDP), the Canada Council for the Arts, and the British Columbia Arts Council.

The author would also like to thank the Canada Council for their generous support during the writing of this book.

Design and typesetting: John van der Woude
Cover Artwork: Getty Images
Printed and bound in Canada

Orca Book Publishers
Box 5626 Station B
Victoria, BC Canada
V8R 6S4

Orca Book Publishers
PO Box 468
Custer, WA USA
98240-0468

08 07 06 05 04 • 6 5 4 3 2 1

For Sam, of course—
because without her (and the outfits)
I would not have survived adolescence at all.

prologue

They had called her *Dog for years already, since kindergarten. Back then she'd come to school every day with a black felt tail pinned to the bum of her pants and floppy ears glued to a headband. When she was five, she wanted to be a dog more than anything. That's when Shadow was just a puppy, a small tumbly thing stumbling over his big paws as he followed her to school, where he whined all day by the fence, waiting for her. When April was five, she loved being called Dog. When she was five, she was popular. All the kids wanted a dog just like Shadow, a dog that never left your side, a dog that would save you from drowning, a dog that would sleep with you every night, his drooly black head on the pillow beside yours. All the kids wanted to be her friend because of Shadow.*

Not anymore. At fourteen, kids were just as likely to call her Bitch, which just naturally progressed out of Dog. They were chanting Dog, though, the day the fire alarm went off during lunch.

Beck shoved April onto her knees as soon as Mr. Cromwell disappeared around the side of the school to find out what was going on and where all the other teachers were. Lindsay held April's arms behind her back, pulling them so tight April thought her collarbone might crack.

"Dog! Dog! Dog!" Half the school crowded her, screaming at her.

Heather pulled a box of dog treats out of her backpack and forced the first one into April's mouth. April had no choice but to chew and swallow; Lindsay was there to bash her face in if she didn't. Heather, Beck, Janika and Jazz all took turns forcing the chalky biscuits down April's throat while the crowd counted.

"Sixteen!"

"Seventeen!"

"She likes them!" Beck hollered. "She used to have them in her lunchbox every day!" That was true, but they were cookies her mom made, shaped like doggie treats because that's how April wanted them, just like Shadow's.

"Twenty!"

"Twenty-one!"

April's throat constricted, but she didn't throw up, not until the box was empty, the crowd had scattered and she was halfway back to class. She threw up in the middle of the hall, outside English. As she retched, someone kicked a garbage can towards her, so she puked in that. She'd eaten the whole box. Fifty-two liver-flavored dog biscuits shaped like bones, and the crumbs at the bottom too.

At five, she prayed to God that she would wake up one day and be a real dog just like Shadow. At fourteen, she prayed to God she'd never wake up at all.

3

zoe

Once again, it was Zoe who got Cassy up. That little brat started screaming her head off just past dawn, jumping around in her crib so it banged against Zoe's bedroom wall, hollering her head off, cheeks red, face covered in snot, and Alice was just across the hall, both doors open, fast asleep? Zoe did not believe her mother could sleep through that. It's humanly impossible. She pretended to, just so Zoe would get up and do it, and then Alice would wander down hours later, when it was too hot to sleep anyway. She'd run her fingers through her hair, yawning while she talked, saying things like, "Oh, what time did you and

Cassy get up?" or "Aw, thanks hon, I was so tired last night I would've slept through a terrorist attack." Alice thought that was funny. Zoe did not.

Cassy screamed even harder when Zoe came into the room that morning. When she did that, Zoe wanted to smack her. Instead, she poked Cassy's belly hard.

"Shut up!"

Her baby sister, half-sister if she was being specific, did shut up. She hiccupped back a great big sob and stretched out her arms to be picked up by her fifteen-year-old fairy princess, her Zo-Zo, who she loved best in the world, after Alice mostly, but not always, sometimes even more than Alice.

Alice knew exactly how to make a bad day even worse. She eventually did get up, just as Zoe was about to take Cassy upstairs and dump her on her, asleep or not. She shuffled around in the kitchen for a while, opening and closing cupboards while Zoe made a great production of leaving. Then when she was halfway down the block, Alice rushed out of the house after her, barefoot, housecoat flapping, tits bouncing under her slip, Cassy pinned under one arm.

"Wait, hon! Come back a minute!"

"I don't have a minute."

"Sure you do." She pulled Zoe back towards the house. "It'll just take a sec."

She steered Zoe into a chair at the kitchen table, in front of a mug of hot lemon tea. Alice sat across from her, fixing her with that honey-I'm-so-sorry look, and inched the sugar in her direction.

"It's too hot for tea." Zoe pushed the sugar back at her.

"I would've made iced tea, but I wanted to catch you before you left."

"You didn't. I'd already left. You know, you could just tell me you want to talk. We don't have to do this every time." Zoe pushed the mug of tea away too. "Can you get on with it? I'm going to be late."

"Okay. All right. Here's the thing." Alice took a sip from her own mug of black coffee. "I got offered a promotion, to manager of the homeless shelter—"

"That's great, Mom! When do—"

"—in Abbotsford, Zoe."

Zoe stared at Alice. Alice stared at the crack on her mug. Outside, the ice cream truck passed on its first round of the day, its looping jingle drawing Cassy to the front door.

"You took it, didn't you?" Zoe pushed her chair back and stood, hands on hips. "You took the job and you never told me? You never even asked what the hell I think about it?"

"Hold on, Zoe, let's talk this out."

"What's there to talk out, huh? If I say I'm sick and tired of moving and want to stay here just TWO MORE YEARS, just until I finish school, would you change your mind?"

"No. I won't lie to you about that."

Zoe hated it when Alice said that, like she was doing Zoe some kind of favor. Like she was all high-and-mighty making some kind of sacrifice by telling the truth.

"I'm going to work now, do you mind?"

"You don't have anything else you want to say about this?"

"Umm, lemmee see." Zoe cocked her head to the side and put a finger to her chin. "Gee, thanks for all that childhood stability, Mom. I'm sure it'll help me develop into a normal, healthy young adult with great self-esteem."

"Sarcasm isn't helpful, Zoe."

"Yeah, well, neither are you." Zoe slammed out the door, even though it'd been open all night because of the heat. She flounced down the sidewalk to find Cassy standing in the middle of the street, waving at the ice cream truck. It idled in front of her, the driver shaking his head in disgust. Behind the toddler, a mini-van full of mothers and children dressed for a day at the lake were just about to pull over and take charge. Zoe narrowed her eyes at the prim-lipped women. She picked Cassy up and dumped her over the fence, hollering at the house, "Come get your kid before the Dickie Dee man runs her over!"

The woman driving the van leaned out her window and curled a finger at Zoe. Zoe held up a hand.

"Save it, lady," she said and then took off through the neighbor's driveway to the alley.

When Zoe came home between the matinees, Alice was taking lasagna out of the oven, face glistening with sweat, a fan set up on either end of the counter, churning the hot stale air.

"You think making my favorite meal will just magically make it all better?"

"Honey—"

"Because it won't." Cassy pulled at Zoe's Movieville-issue shorts with chocolate-batter hands. Zoe picked her up and carried her to the sink, holding her away from the stupid yellow shirt with the film reel on the back. She rinsed Cassy's hands under the tap. "Brownies, too? If you feel this bad maybe it means you're doing something wrong. Did you ever think about that? That maybe you made a mistake?"

"It's not a mistake." Alice wiped her brow with an oven mitt. "Look, I'm sorry you're taking it so hard, but—"

"How else am I supposed to take it?"

"As an opportunity for positive change, Zoe."

That, right there, was Alice Diane Anderson's answer to everything since she'd started borrowing self-help tapes from the library. You cut your leg off with a chainsaw? Hell, that's no biggie, look at it as an opportunity for positive change! Your child was kidnapped and raped by the vacuum salesman? Well, gosh, let's not say she's scarred for life; let's say she's been given the opportunity for positive change! Oh, he left her dead in a ditch? Well then it's your opportunity for positive change, isn't it?

The only positive thing Zoe could conceive about moving, and she would never tell Alice this, she wouldn't want to give her the satisfaction, is that she would be glad to see the ass-end of Prince George. If Vancouver was Hollywood North, with its cappuccino and production studios, its sea-wall dotted with celebrities, the ocean breeze washing the city with slick, fresh appeal, then Prince George was the capital of lame home movies shown on stained white sheets tacked to basement fake-wood paneling, grainy shots of naked babies waving in bathtubs and humiliating slices of school plays.

Prince George was full of 4X4-ing, hockey addicted, sweat-drenched guys whose sole goal in life was to get on at the mill and save up for a big screen TV. And their girlfriends, we can't forget about those skanks, with their biffed-up hair and skin-tight jeans and high heels and Budweiser tank tops. Zoe's Prince George littermates wouldn't know there was any different way of being, even if they were abducted by aliens in the middle of one of their bush parties and deposited, alone, in various cities all over the world. They'd just sit on the curb, light a cigarette or roll a joint and wait for their beer-guzzling buddies to show up to drive them to the rink.

On the other hand, Zoe had been fully prepared to stick it out there until she graduated, although since Luisa went back to Brazil, she was friendless again. The summers were always like that. The next exchange student wouldn't come until September. Zoe was already looking forward to that. Before Luisa, Milo and Jane down the street had sponsored Natasha from Russia, and before her, Perseverance from Haiti. Zoe counted on their supply of exotic girls from far-off places to fill the rotating role of Zoe's Best Friend, otherwise she would never have any friends at all.

The way Zoe looked at it, all the lamevilles she'd ever lived in were material for her to use later, not that she intended to make movies about dumpy towns in the middle of nowhere, but enduring them, *that* would make her a better filmmaker.

Every creative genius had a shitty childhood they grew up to exploit, right?

This would be, let's see...Kamloops, Trail, Vernon, Grand Forks, Lethbridge—if you count that three month "This is it, Zoe, he's so good to us and I'm totally in love" disaster—Kelowna, Williams Lake, Prince George and now Abbotsford. Nine moves in fifteen years, and not one of them to anywhere half decent. Was that fair?

Oh, but wait, we all know what Alice would say to that.

"Whoever said life was fair, Zoe? Did I ever say life was fair? Now I know I've said a lot of things about life, but I never said it was fair, did I?" No, she never did, but that didn't mean she was right. It just meant she knew how to rework tired old parental clichés.

moving day

For Zoe and Alice, moving day normally looked like this: Alice screaming at Zoe from inside the U-haul, did you pack this or that and do you know where the whatsit is and could you bloody well hurry it up 'cuz we don't have all day, you know? And Zoe, running up and down the walk with boxes and chairs and lamps and suitcases and black garbage bags full of stuff they ran out of time to pack properly. They always left a whole pile at the end of the driveway with a Free sign, either because they ran out of time, or they ran out of room, or it was junk they didn't want anymore anyway.

This move was different. The Fraser Valley Regional Homeless Shelter and Housing Resource Society, thankfully called Fraser House by most, was paying for the move. Alice and Zoe just lounged in their bathing suits and sunglasses on towels on the front lawn, lathered in suntan lotion. Zoe guzzled back lemonade in the dry heat, while Alice sipped hers, generously spiked with mint schnapps. All they had to do was pick up lunch for the road and make sure Cassy didn't end up packed in a crate. She was determined to help. She'd hooked her beloved purple plastic dinosaur cup on one thumb and was pushing boxes down the hall three times as big as her, grunting and muttering, "Cassy do it, Cassy do it," until one of the movers gave her the job of sitting on a stool beside the door holding a "very important" empty tape gun.

Just as the three of them were about to leave, Harris drove up, his beat-up truck clunking so loud they heard him long before they saw him.

Alice pulled her sunglasses down briefly. "Here we go," she muttered under her breath. "Prepare for a scene."

Harris had come over late the night before, after Zoe had finally finished packing and had gone to bed. She'd been asleep, but his truck woke her up. He and Alice had talked in the kitchen with the door closed, their voices starting out all hushed and civilized and then getting louder and louder until they were screaming at each other like afternoon talk show trash.

He was all, "What the hell makes you think you can just up and take off with my little girl?"

And Alice was all, "You knew damn well when we got into this that I wasn't making you no promises! You didn't even want her in the first place, and now it's breaking your heart to see her go? You think I'm some kind of idiot? You think I'm that stupid?"

There was a dangerous pause, and then something, it sounded like a beer bottle, smashed onto the tiles. Harris hollered at Alice that he'd see her in court; she hollered back at him that if he was that organized she'd be damned surprised, and then he slammed out the back door so hard it bounced back on its springs three times.

The next morning, he'd switched to a different tactic—begging, complete with a dozen yellow roses, a little wilted from the heat.

"Alice?" he hollered from his truck. "Alice!" The movers squinted into the sun at him. Harris scowled at them. "What the hell you looking at?"

Alice shook her head. "You, you stupid idiot!"

Harris's mouth gawped open, like he was going to tear into Alice for that. Zoe could almost see him reeling in the nasties, as if they were on fishing line, until all he said was, "Don't I even get a chance to change your mind?"

"No, you do not, Harris Kellerman!"

Harris knocked his forehead against the steering wheel a couple of times before getting out and marching over. He must've done the night shift after their fight; he reeked of the cannery, fish and sweat. He thrust the roses at her. "I'm just asking you to reconsider, Alice. Please?"

"No." Alice set the roses on the grass beside her.

"Come on, baby. Please? Think about it? Humor me? At least keep it in mind?"

"Keep what in mind?" Zoe asked.

"It doesn't matter, Zoe." Alice sighed. "Harris, we've been through this a hundred times, and this is just the way it is. See that?" She pointed to the moving truck. "That's going to drive all our things to Abbotsford. And see that?" She pointed to the orange station wagon, with its bashed-in side and mismatched hood. "That's going to take my little family to Abbotsford. My little family: Zoe, Cassy and me."

"That's not fair, Alice." Harris put a hand above his eyes, shielding the sun.

Zoe looked at Alice, eyebrows raised, waiting for her to give him the whoever-said-life-was-fair line. Alice just stared at him, waiting for him to get on with it.

"There's nothing I can say? Nothing I can do?"

Alice shook her head.

"Alice." He pointed a nicotine-stained finger at her. "You're one hell of a hard woman, you know that?"

"It's a free country." Alice shrugged. "Think whatever you want."

"Jesus." Harris shook his head. "At least tell me you'll think about it?"

"I am not going to lie to you just because that's what you want to hear." Alice's tone was fast shifting from just barely tolerant to right pissed off.

"Okay, okay." He stepped back, hands up. "I give up, then. Obviously that's what you want."

He waited for Alice to argue with that, but she just lit a cigarette and said nothing. Cassy toddled down the steps with her tape dispenser and plunked herself on Alice's lap. Harris stared at the two of them and sighed. He leaned down and kissed Cassy on the top of her head and Alice on her cheek. He would've kissed her on the lips, but she turned her head at the last second. He looked the three of them up and down, and then placed his hand on Cassy's head, feeling her soft curls and the sweaty heat of her, until Cassy grabbed onto his thick fingers and pushed him away.

"See ya, kid." He opened his arms to Zoe.

Zoe hugged him, not because she was sad to see the last of him, but because she felt sorry for him, the way Alice was brushing him off, and Cassy too, like none of them ever really wanted him in the first place. For a second, Zoe felt bad about all the things she wrote about him in her diary, like the way he stank of fish all the time, and how he just barged in without knocking, and the way he yelled at Cassy if she came anywhere near his beer or cigarettes or Prince George Pirates hat. She watched him drive off real slow, stepping on the brakes more than necessary, and then she and Alice packed up the car and Cassy and left, taking the long way to the highway so they wouldn't pass his house on the way.

abbotsford

Abbotsford smelled like cow shit, thanks to the surrounding farms. The small city was blanketed in a disgusting yellow smog that crept down the valley from Vancouver like a slow mob of foul ghosts, but worst of all was that the small city was full of the same boring crap as Prince George: fast food chains, rundown motels, gas stations, car dealerships, boarded-up shops and a half empty strip mall every ten blocks or so. The only difference Zoe noted at first, and it was rather alarming, was that there were so many churches it looked like religion was the industry, like Abbotsford's claim to international trade fame was producing factory-model Christians for waning congregations all over the world: perfect, tidy, wide-grinning Jesus freaks of all shapes and colors.

Rejoice In His Name, the mother lode of all churches—the parking lot alone took up two square blocks—was just down the road from their new place. It had a hundred-foot-high white neon cross cabled up on the roof that Zoe could see from the crusty, rather un-Christian motel they spent their first night at, and it was all the way out by the highway.

As for the first person she met, that did not go well. While Alice went to get the key at Paradise Heights, a scabby condo complex that was not paradise and was not high up to anything, Zoe and Cassy found a little playground, and there she was: perched at the top of the jungle gym, stocky, about Zoe's age, short auburn hair stuck up all over on purpose, olive green cargo shorts, black tank top, a cigarette pinched between her first and second fingers like a joint, bare feet dangling over the edge, a pair of skater shoes and a puddle of butts on the ground under her.

Cassy tilted her head back to look up at her. The girl frowned down, took a drag off her cigarette and flicked it onto the sand at Cassy's feet, barely missing her head. Cassy squatted and peered at it. She carefully set down her dinosaur cup and reached out to pick up the smoldering butt.

"Cassy, no!" Zoe yanked her away. She glared up at the girl. "What the hell did you do that for?"

She shrugged. "I didn't see her."

"You looked right at her!"

The girl shrugged again, and then pushed herself off her perch. She was at least eight feet up, but she landed smoothly on both feet. She narrowed her eyes and tilted her head back just so, all tough-girl slick.

"I said I didn't see her." She took a deliberate step forward.

"Like hell you didn't see her." Zoe turned to leave with Cassy. She might rag on her little sister a bit, but the fact remained that she was more of a mama bear than Alice would ever be when it came to Cassy. "What a bitch."

The girl clamped a hand on Zoe's shoulder. "Look, if you want to make this a big deal, go right ahead, little girl."

"Little girl?" Zoe was taller than she was, by a good two inches. "She must be talking to you, Cassy," Zoe baby talked at her. "What do you say? You wanna make a big deal, honey?"

The girl tensed. She lifted her arm slightly, like she was either going to push her bangs out of her eyes or belt Zoe in the face, but before she could do either, Alice came down the path and called for Zoe and Cassy to come see the new place.

Number eleven Paradise Heights smelled like stale bedding and pork chops. Zoe's new room stank of stale bedding, pork chops and cat pee. Kid scribbles decorated all four walls.

"We can paint as soon as there's some extra cash," Alice said, lingering at the door.

Zoe didn't even bother to nod. She just added the suggestion to the very long list of things Alice said they could do as soon as there was some extra cash.

Alice took a small step into the room. "Where're you going to put your travelling star?"

Zoe was six when Alice first brought the traveling stars home halfway through the school year, a few days after Alice had announced she'd got a job in Grand Forks that started in a month. Zoe told her mother that if she left her a loaf of bread and a jar of peanut butter and some apples, she'd stay behind and live in the garden shed and go to school on time every day and wouldn't bother the new renters at all. Alice said she'd think about it.

The next day, she brought home a handful of plastic glow-in-the-dark stars wrapped in a square of purple silk. She said they were travelling stars, given to her by the moving fairy, who thought it'd be a bad idea for Zoe to live in the shed all by herself.

According to Alice, the fairy put a spell on them, so they'd capture all the good stuff from Vernon and carry it to their new place in Grand Forks. After that, whenever they moved, they were the last thing to come down, and the first to go up, a ritual, which up until now, Zoe had always looked forward to.

Usually she'd wander around any new bedroom, trailing her fingers along the walls, waiting for the perfect spot to speak to her, but this time she just reached up from where she was sitting and stuck one on the wall. Maybe it'd lost its magic, or maybe there was no good stuff to bring from Prince George. Or maybe it was just a stupid ritual to placate little kids.

Alice frowned at it, lopsided in the corner. She pointed her beer bottle at it. "You can pick a better place for it once we've painted."

Zoe didn't want to pick a better place. She wanted to pluck it off the wall and chuck it out the window along with all the other trash out there rotting on the carport roof.

"We're going to be fine, Zoe." Alice touched the star, as if for good luck. "I just know it. This move is a great opportunity for positive change. You've just got to—"

"Give it a chance," Zoe cut her off. "I know."

Later, while Alice looked through the phone book for a motel to stay at for the night, Zoe pushed open her window, careful to brace the cracked glass. She climbed out onto the carport roof and stepped around the trash to the edge. She stared into the night, past the blue TV shimmer of rooms lit behind curtains, over the roofs and across to the little playground.

The girl was still there, on a swing, pumping hard, so high the chain slackened before letting her down. Then suddenly she stopped, digging her bare feet into the sand. There was a tiny flash of flame as she lit a cigarette, the tip bright orange as she inhaled. She kicked herself in circles, tightening the chain until it wouldn't turn anymore. Then for a second, she stared across the night between them and right at Zoe until she let go, spinning into a dark fast blur.

17

first day of school

The next time Zoe saw the girl was on the first day of school. Her name was Beck, short for Rebecca, and she was definitely what Alice would call "a piece of work." Zoe was herded into the gym that first morning along with all the other new students to get paired up with someone who was supposed to show them around. Mr. Cromwell, the fat counselor in charge, called them "volunteer ambassadors." Most of them looked like factory-fresh Christians, with perfect haircuts and preppy clothes, the girls with careful lipstick, the boys with polished shoes and buttoned-up shirts tucked in; but some of them obviously did not want to be there, including Beck, who strolled in while Mr. Cromwell blathered on about the school's district-wide famous zero tolerance policy on drugs.

"So nice of you to join us." He frowned at her. "I was looking for you."

She mimicked his frown. "You found me. Congratulations."

He pointed a shut-up finger at her, and finished with his threats of expulsion and police involvement. Then he started down the list, pairing them off. He called Zoe's name and Beck's in the same breath. Up in the bleachers, Zoe slowly stood. Not really. Not her. No way.

"Not her, Cromwell." Beck shook her head. "Just this one little favor?"

Cromwell waved for Zoe to hurry up.

"And you," he said to Zoe when she joined them, "Wipe that look off your face. You're too new to have grudges." He checked Zoe's name on the list. "Rebecca." He snapped his fingers. "Get over here, pronto."

"Don't call me that." She pushed herself away from the wall and sauntered over, glaring at Zoe. When Mr. Cromwell looked up from the roster, Beck smiled at him. "Come on, Cromwell. Don't do this to me." She hooked an arm through his. "I'm the last person she wants to hang out with."

"All the more reason, then." Cromwell removed her arm and handed them each a piece of paper. "You two can work it out. This is Zoe's schedule." He looked over his glasses at Beck. "And if I hear you've ditched Miss Anderson at any point during the day, we'll be having words, or more to the point *I'll* be having words and *you* will be sitting in a chair listening attentively."

Zoe walked a couple paces behind Beck as she led her all over the school, like Zoe was some half-wit who wouldn't realize what she was doing.

"Come on." Zoe was not about to go back down the stairs they'd just come up. "Are you taking me there or not?"

"Oh, look, we're there." Beck pointed down the hall at a green door with a Shakespeare poster under the little window. "I'll be back for you after class."

"Don't bother," Zoe said. "It's obvious you don't want to do this. Forget it."

"I said, I'll be back for you after class. If I don't babysit you all day, Cromwell will have my ass, okay? Happy?"

"Why did you volunteer then?"

"I don't *volunteer* to do anything. This is Cromwell's idea of 'rehabilitation.'" She pulled a pack of cigarettes out of her bag and stuck one between her lips before taking off down the stairs.

A tiny woman with a sweep of silver hair piled high on her head opened the door just as Beck disappeared.

"Do tell me you are not going to stand out here all day." Mrs. Henley pulled Zoe into the room by her elbow. "Take a seat, child." Zoe made her way to a desk at the back, thirty sets of who-the-hell-is-*she* eyes locked on her.

"You'll have plenty of time to alienate her later, people." Mrs. Henley picked up a clipboard. "Now, all I ask, please, is that when I call your name you answer anything but *yeah*." She raced through the list, hardly waiting for the "heres" and "presents" until she called out "Rebecca? *Miz* Wilson?" Silence. "Has anyone seen her this morning?" Silence. "No one has seen the illustrious Beck yet?" She looked down her nose at two girls in particular, a chunky blonde with harsh eyebrows, and a tiny South Asian girl with hair down to her bum. "Why do I find that hard to believe?"

Everyone stared blankly forward.

"April? You were in the gym just now, was she there?"

A skinny girl with limp wheat-colored hair looked up from scratching her knees. She turned in her desk to look at Zoe.

Zoe slouched in her seat and looked right through her. April turned back to the front and nodded, lanky hair falling across her narrow face, fingers worrying a gold cross at her throat, a WWJD bracelet slipping down her wrist. Until then, Zoe had thought the whole What-Would-Jesus-Do thing was a joke. She didn't believe people actually wore that crap, let alone believed in it.

"Well? Was she or was she not in the gymnasium with the other volunteer ambassadors?"

The class snickered.

"Yes," April whispered.

"Hark!" Mrs. Henley cupped a hand to her ear. "Is that the sound of verity I hear before me?" She noted something on her clipboard before smiling generously at April. "Thank you, Miz Donelly."

Beck was waiting in the hall after class, although it was only to pass Zoe off to Simon, a pale, slender boy who towered beside her, dressed all in black, from boots to porkpie hat. Beck pushed him forward.

"Simon's taking you to Chemistry."

Simon wiggled his fingers at Zoe. "Hey."

"I have to take off." Beck glanced down the hall. "Pretend Simon is me, except ugly and with a lisp."

"I love you too, sweetheart." Simon scowled at her.

"What about Cromwell?"

"I've got an emergency. If you see Cromwell, tell him I'm busy being bulimic or something."

"Welcome to Central." Simon folded his arms and watched Beck hurry down the hall. "Home of freaks, geeks and mental cases. Just your average run of the mill public educational institution, where chaos reigns supreme." He draped an arm across Zoe's shoulders and led her down the stairs, taking two steps for her one.

"Why'd she take off?"

"Lady Heather slit her wrists again."

"What?" Zoe stopped. "Who did *what*?"

"Heather Arlington-Moore, best friend of Beck, better known in some circles as Central's suicide queen. She had another one of her...how should I put it?" He made quotations with his fingers. "Episodes." He continued down the stairs backwards, perfectly poised as the crowd jostled past him. "She's all right though. She does this all the time. I've told her how to do it properly, but I suppose that's not what she's really after."

"What's she really after?"

"Oh, who knows what goes on in that pretty little head of hers? She does this every once and a while. It's never really serious."

Never really serious? Was *he* serious? Zoe followed Simon to the science wing and into a dim lab at the end of the hall. Mr. Turner, a loafers-and-polyester man who fiddled obsessively with his moustache, hung around just long enough to take attendance and make sure everyone signed for their textbook. That done, he left the room without a word.

"He won't be back." Simon checked his watch. "Time for his mid-morning gin and tonic." He stood. "Coming?"

"Where?"

"I don't know. Smoke hole? Corner store? Home?"

Zoe watched the majority of the class gather their books and leave. "I don't think so."

"Suit yourself." Simon hitched his pack on his shoulder and left too. Zoe stayed, along with a couple other bewildered new students too nervous to leave and two geeks who were already digging into their textbooks, highlighters in hand. Zoe spent the hour writing in her diary, speculating on what exactly might be the correct way to slit your wrists.

the beckoners

Zoe met Central's suicide queen on the second day of school when Simon dragged Zoe out to the smoke hole at lunch. Halfway across the parking lot he stopped mid-stride, opening his arms to the crowd gathered under the trees and around the makeshift hut.

"You've got your skids, your punks, pushers, users, Goths, slags, geeks, hippies, rejects and other standard garden variety misfits—the ones that smoke, at least." He sighed. "Home sweet home."

And then he abandoned her there, out in the open to fend for herself, exposed, every sullen smoker giving her the loaded eye, while he went off to smoke hash in the ravine with his boyfriend, Teo, who just happened to be the most beautiful creature Zoe had ever laid her eyes on. His eyes were dark green, his skin the color of strong tea, muscles humming all over the place, and a walk that absolutely demanded you stare at his ass.

Zoe was distracted for the moment, watching the two of them approach the trail. They were an odd couple: Simon's frenetic gait beside Teo's calm, confident stride.

Zoe could've turned back to the school then, but that would've been tantamount to falling to her knees and screaming, "I'm not worthy!" Hell, she had as much right to be there as anyone else. She took a moment to square her shoulders and then walked confidently forward, as if she knew exactly where she was going, meeting the eyes of every waster who took the time and energy to stare at her.

Beck was sitting at the end table in the hut with a bunch of girls surrounding a supermodel wannabe perched cross-legged on the table, long legs tucked under her, mascara running in two neat black lines down her cheeks. That would be Heather, judging by Simon's description. She tucked a long strawberry blonde curl behind her ear and looked up.

"Yeah?" She managed perfect snob pitch, despite the tears. "What?"

"That's the girl, from yesterday," Beck said.

"Oh." Heather pulled a pack of menthol slims out of a little silver backpack. She held the cigarettes in Zoe's direction. "Want one?"

Zoe shook her head and watched the three other girls vie for the privilege to light Heather's cigarette. She recognized two of them from English, the ones Mrs. Henley had looked down her nose at.

"You seen the smoke hole yet?" Heather swept a slender arm in an arc. "This is the smoke hole." She pointed her cigarette at the girls around the table. "That's Lindsay, Janika, Jasvinder—

we call her Jazz. And you know Beck." Lindsay was the chunky blonde from class. Jazz was the one with the hair to her bum, although today it was in a messy knot at the nape of her neck. Janika was black, with a mass of thin braids held away from her heart-shaped face with a red bandana. Heather widened her eyes at Zoe. "Well, that about covers it. You can go now."

"Right," Zoe muttered, turning to leave. "See ya."

"Hang on." Beck eyed Heather and patted the bench. "Have a seat. What's your name again?"

"Zoe." Zoe did not want to sit down. She'd only come into the hut so she could turn right back around and saunter out like she hadn't found who she was looking for. But you don't walk away from girls like this. You don't turn your back on girls like this unless you're prepared for them to slice you wide open, and not necessarily right away—girls like this were brilliant at simmering resentments. Zoe sat down.

"What are you *doing*, Beck?" Heather tapped her ash off the edge of the concrete table.

Beck ignored her. "So, where're you from?"

"Prince George."

"I don't like her." Heather narrowed her eyes at Zoe. She unfolded her legs and nudged Beck's shoulder with her Paris knock-off wedge sandal. "I'm talking to you. I said I don't like her. Get rid of her."

"I went to Prince George once." Beck pushed Heather's foot away. "Or we went through it, on the way to my aunt's wedding in Terrace." Then she said, "Hey, what would you've done if your mom hadn't come the other day?"

"Kicked your head in," Zoe blurted. Nobody laughed. Jazz, Lindsay and Janika all turned to Beck, waiting for a reaction.

"Oh, I am so sure." Heather rolled her eyes.

"Kicked my head in?" Beck cocked her head to one side and sized Zoe up with a new respect. "Is that so?"

No, that was not so. Zoe stifled a laugh. She glanced at Heather, who was sucking furiously on her cigarette.

Like hell, Zoe would've kicked Beck's head in. She was being funny. It's called sarcasm. She used it a lot when she was nervous, and it had gotten her in trouble more than once. In real life, she would've run. She would've run as fast and as far as she could, with Cassy weighing her down.

Zoe took a breath.

"How about you?" Always a good tactic, answer a question with a question. "What were you going to do?"

"God, spare us the encoded speech." Heather stubbed out her cigarette.

Still, Beck didn't look at her. She pulled out her own cigarettes, lit one and then offered the pack to Zoe. "Want one?"

"She doesn't smoke." Heather scowled at Beck. "Were, or were you not here when I very nicely offered her one two minutes ago?"

"I don't smoke menthols," Zoe said. She'd had enough of Heather's almighty bullshit. Taking a cigarette from Beck would piss Heather off nicely. Retaliation could be so subtle.

It was extremely important to take the cigarette from Beck anyway. It was as if they'd reached some kind of peace treaty that depended on it. Heather huffed dramatically as Zoe put the cigarette between her lips.

Beck flipped open a pack of matches with an eight ball on the cover and lit the cigarette for her, letting the smallest edges of what you could call a smile soften her face.

Thank you, Luisa, for teaching Zoe how to smoke on the field trip to the petroglyphs last year. The girls all watched to see if she was really inhaling. Zoe felt the familiar cough tickle her throat, but she swallowed it back.

"You can still leave now." Heather pointed her cigarette at the door. "Did I mention where the door is, during your little escorted tour of the smoke hole just now?"

"Thanks for the cigarette." Zoe started to get up, but Beck put a hand on her arm and finally looked up at Heather.

"Stop it, Heather."

"Stop what?" Heather surveyed the others. "We were having a private conversation, which she interrupted and now I just want to get back to it. Is that okay with everyone? Could we do that? Or are we going to start handing out cigarettes to every dog who comes begging?"

"Of course not, baby." Janika put an arm around Heather and shot Zoe a pointed look that said "let that one go, girl." Zoe swallowed back the comeback she was working up like spit in her mouth. "Start from where she cut you off."

"Thank you, *Janika*." Heather scowled at Beck, and then launched back into her sob story, which was, Zoe guessed, the causal factor in suicide attempt number whatever, something about her boyfriend Brady cheating on her with some grade nine slut from another school when they'd been broken up for a couple of days the week before.

Simon, as high as that neon cross on the Rejoice In His Name roof, rescued Zoe before she'd even finished the cigarette. He pulled her away, stealing the last half of the smoke and sharing it with Teo. He and Teo hooked Zoe's arms and escorted her past the jury members, who'd decided a verdict wasn't called for, considering Beck's involvement. They crossed the street and cut through Paradise Heights to the corner store, where they bought two ice cream sandwiches each, and one for Zoe.

"Looks like the Beckoners got their claws in you already," Teo said through a mouthful of ice cream. "You watch out, girl."

"Why?"

"They are some nasty bitches." Simon pinched her butt. "You just watch your flat little ass, if you're going to play with the Beckoners."

"The Beckoners?"

"Beck's little girly gang. You know. Beck. Beckon. The Beckoners."

"Doesn't matter if you beckon or not, they come calling when they want." Teo broke into giggles. He leaned over and kissed Simon on the lips. Simon kissed him back, just as a carload of jocks drove by, hollering "faggot" out the windows. The boys and Zoe all flipped them the finger.

After they turned the corner, Simon said, "For a northern hick, you're pretty cool about queers."

"There's queers up north too, you know." Zoe shrugged. For a time, Zoe had wondered if she might be gay herself. She'd kissed Luisa lots of times, each sleepover ended up with Luisa suggesting they "practice." Luisa pouted if Zoe wouldn't go along with it, so Zoe took the rather long, drawn-out sloppy opportunity to survey how she was feeling. It was okay. Kind of nice. Gross, though, that one time they'd had Caesar salad for supper. She didn't get turned on though, but then again, maybe Luisa wasn't her type.

Zoe wasn't about to tell them about Luisa, so instead she said, "Besides, who wouldn't think Teo is a catch?"

"I like this one." Teo grabbed her face in his hands and kissed her on the lips. "Let's keep her." Even though she knew he was into boys, Zoe couldn't help but notice her belly did an enthusiastic back flip. He was a much better kisser than Luisa, that was for sure.

On the way back to the school they passed April, coming back from her house. She lived in Paradise Heights too, number twenty-two. Shadow, eleven years old now and with arthritic hips, trotted as best he could beside her, tail wagging. Zoe lifted her hand to wave, but Simon grabbed it.

"Nuh uh, don't even go there. That's Dog."

"April?" Zoe squinted at her. "She's in my English class."

"Her name is Dog." Simon pulled Zoe along. "She's a total loser. Don't go anywhere near her, or she'll get on you."

simon says

One thing about Simon that set him apart from everyone Zoe had ever met, was his ability to leap on a tangent and fly away. Teo called these tangents "Simon's verbal seizures." Simon called them "essential thoughts and information on important subjects." Zoe called them "Simon Says" moments.

Like the one about Dog's notebook: that ratty old exercise book she carried with her everywhere, usually folded in half in her back pocket, so worn at the crease it was reinforced with duct tape twice over.

"See that?" Simon pointed it out as Dog passed them in the hall one day.

"Her butt?"

"No. The notebook." He leaned closer and whispered. "That's *the* notebook."

"*The* notebook?" Zoe shrugged. "The notebook I should be aware of because…?"

"You know what would be really helpful?" Simon said to Teo.

"Here we go," Teo muttered. "I sense a verbal seizure coming on."

"What would be really helpful is if new students got implanted with some sort of microchip that held all the gossip about their new school, so that people like me wouldn't have to go over and over it."

"A microchip?"

"*Yes,* because if you had such a thing implanted in your head, then you would know the importance of that notebook and I wouldn't have to tell you all about it."

"It's okay, Simon, you don't have to."

"Good." Simon smiled. "I'm glad."

"No, you're not," Teo said.

"Yes, I am." Simon took a deep breath. "It's a relief." He looked at Teo, who was staring at him, eyebrows raised. "What are you looking at?"

"The rest of the seizure. You're not done yet."

Simon eyed Zoe. "You really don't want to know about the notebook?"

Zoe shrugged. "Doesn't matter."

"You see?" He gripped her shoulders. "That's where you're wrong! How can you know about anything if you don't know about it *all*? Okay, that notebook for example. It's like Dog's inventory, of all the things people do to her. I've seen it. It's crammed with all this teeny tiny writing right out to the edges of the paper, like some kind of schizophrenic manifesto. You know, I wouldn't be surprised if she ends up being schizophrenic. She's weird like that, like who else believes all that immaculate conception, resurrection crap unless they're delusional?"

"Most of Abbotsford, Simon," Teo said.

"My point. Anyway, little miss Christianity goes to that happy clappy church—"

"Rejoice In His Name," Teo supplied.

"Repent for your Shame," Simon muttered. "So, last year Cromwell starts going there too. And he sits in the pew right behind her and they do that whole shake hands, 'Jesus loves you, my friend' stuff every Sunday. Well, guess what?" Simon didn't leave room for an answer. "Dog developed a soft spot for Cromwell and starts writing about him, in *the* notebook, how she looks forward to seeing him every Sunday, and what blue eyes he has and how he's so sweet always wearing those funny suspenders her little brother likes. She goes on and on about how kind he is, how much she likes him, what a nice man he is, even if he's so fat one less person than usual can fit in the pew. Oh! Oh, the best, the *best* is how she feels so sorry for him that he has no girlfriend. She's like, 'He's probably a great lover and a marvelous kisser, to make up for what he lacks in physique.' Oh. My. God."

"Her God," Teo muttered.

"Her god? I don't know if I would call it her god, seeing as how her god did nothing to stop Lindsay from stealing the notebook right out of Dog's back pocket in the cafeteria lineup one day. *Her* god didn't stop the Beckoners from passing it around for days, using a magnifying glass to read her miniscule writing. I bet you Dog was on her knees begging Jesus for a miracle, like the book would spontaneously combust or something."

"The whole thing is cruel," Zoe said.

"It gets worse," Simon said.

"Much worse," Teo said.

Simon continued. "The Beckoners photocopied and enlarged bits of it, cutting and pasting. They made a poster that said, in Dog's own writing, with her very own signature at the bottom: 'I love Cromwell, his soft kiss, his blue eyes, his flesh against mine.'"

"That's so mean!" Zoe put a hand over her mouth. She watched Dog disappear into a room at the end of the hallway. Poor pathetic her.

"Yeah, it is, but you know what's worse? They made two hundred copies and pasted them up beside another poster, one that showed April and Cromwell kissing. They'd taken a photo of her, side profile, and a photo of him, side profile, and doctored them on the computer so it looked like they were kissing like porn stars."

"I would die," Zoe said.

"Yeah, so would most people, but she didn't even transfer schools. Those things were everywhere: lining the halls, the windows, papering Cromwell's door, on the fence around the school. And she didn't even miss one class, let alone quit or transfer or bomb the school."

"I would've killed myself," Zoe said.

"And that would've been a very reasonable response," Simon said.

Teo whacked him on the shoulder. "Don't even say that."

"Well, it's truc. Pcople kill themselves over a lot less. All I'm saying is I wouldn't blame her. Would you blame her?"

Teo shook his head. "But Christians don't kill themselves, right? They go to hell if they do."

"And I ask you, what would be worse? Being Dog here on earth or rotting in hell?"

Zoe and Teo glanced at each other.

Zoe shrugged. "I don't know much about hell."

"At least hell's run by an ex-angel. Beck's always been Beck," Teo said.

"No, she hasn't." Simon's tone softened. "But that's another subject."

"Another seizure, more like it." Teo took Zoe's hand. "Just don't ask. If you don't ask, sometimes the seizures don't happen."

"I didn't ask anything just now."

Teo whispered, "Sometimes they just can't be helped."

This time Simon whacked Teo. "Subtle."

"Unlike you." Teo whacked him back. "Are you done?"

Simon tilted his head to the side and considered the matter. "Yeah, I guess."

"So she got a different notebook?" Zoe marveled, realizing. "After all that, and she got another notebook?"

"Some dogs never learn," said Simon. "Others do. I heard Cromwell doesn't even go to Repent for your Shame anymore."

breaking glass

It was Friday the thirteenth, or early morning Saturday, really, when Zoe woke up to the sound of glass smashing, lots of it, so much that it sounded like it was pouring out the back of a dump truck. She wondered at first if she was really still asleep and this was one of those real-not-real dreams. People were shouting, but she couldn't make out what they were saying. Alice came into her room, pulling on her robe.

"What the hell is that?"

They looked out the window, but all they could see were other people looking out their windows. Cassy started fussing in

Alice's room, but Alice wasn't budging, so Zoe went to her. She picked her up and was going to take her into her room, but then she glanced out Alice's window and froze. The Beckoners were running along the trail through the brambles in the vacant lot behind Paradise Heights. They stopped under the streetlight at the far corner, the bright pink of Heather's jacket standing out in the night like a stuffed toy tossed from a car.

Earlier that day, Mrs. Henley had told them about Virginia Woolf walking into the river with her pockets full of rocks, drowning from the weight of them. When Zoe fell back asleep, Cassy warm and sweaty beside her, she dreamt of the Beckoners with their pockets sagging and stretching with stones, the five of them walking in a line down a smooth beach and into the surf of a strange violent sea, all of them drowning like Virginia Woolf, their bodies washing to shore in a jumble of bloated arms and legs.

The next morning, after Alice left for work, Zoe put Cassy in the stroller and went to investigate. The breaking glass had sounded like it came from somewhere above the playground.

It was Dog's house. She was in the carport, picking glass off the hood of a rusting minivan with leather gloves that were too big for her. An ambulance was parked behind the van. Shadow was tied up by the front door, whining, eyes fixed on Dog.

Dog looked at Zoe for a second, eyes wounded and accusing, and then she turned back to the van. The Beckoners had made a terrible mess. All the van windows had been smashed, even the little triangle windows near the back, as well as every single window of their house. The way the curtains billowed out it looked like the windows had been flung open to let the fresh autumn air in. On the grass and pavement below, the glass sparkled with dew, glinting in the sunshine like a spill of jewels. A little boy in a gray sweatsuit and a red plastic firefighter's hat pushed a wide broom he could hardly manage down the path towards Zoe, spreading the glass along further.

"Lewis, get back here!" Barb, the pear-shaped lady who ran Cassy's daycare, chased after him. She hauled him away from the glass. "Go inside and watch cartoons, would you?" She kissed the top of his head and pushed him towards the house.

"Mom, the can's full." Dog eyed Zoe again.

Barb was Dog's mom? Barb, who was so cotton candy happy-happy in her pastel tracksuits with appliquéd bible scenes, her fluffy hair, her apple soap scent perfuming the air around her like she was a real-life scratch-and-sniff sticker? Dog was so flat, so drippy. Everything about her was limp: her clothes, her hair, her smell, like tired lettuce left out in the heat.

"Well, dump it then," Barb said.

Dog clutched the garbage can, eyes on Zoe like she was considering dumping the glass over Zoe's head.

"Oh, for heaven's sake, give it to me." Barb took the can from her. That's when she noticed Zoe. She smiled wide. "Oh, Zoe! Didn't even see you there, watch out, dear." She pushed past her. "Coming through. You know April?" Barb didn't wait for Zoe to answer. "April, this is Zoe. Alice's other girl. You know Alice. Cassy's mommy? Zoe, this is my daughter, April." Barb dumped the glass, the clatter echoing against the metal walls of the dumpster parked on their little patch of grass.

"We're in English together," Zoe said. It was true. It was safe. She stared at the ambulance. "Did someone get hurt?"

"Oh, thank the good Lord, no. April's daddy is a paramedic. Sometimes he comes home with it." Barb pulled off her gloves. "He's upstairs sleeping off a night shift." She undid Cassy's belt and lifted her into her arms, nibbling her belly, rubbing noses. Cassy grabbed a fist of Barb's sandy curls and held tight.

Dog and Zoe stared at each other. Barb kept babbling.

"Can you believe *I* had Mrs. Henley when I was your age? That was when the school was two wooden buildings in the corner of the football field. It burnt down in 1978. That was something to see. I've got pictures of it. I'll get my yearbooks."

The year before, Zoe had taken First Aid, and they had talked about shock, which Zoe had been surprised to find out was an actual physiological collapse. She'd always thought when people went into shock, it was like Barb that morning, babbling on with a retard grin, in complete denial that every single window of her house had been deliberately bashed in. She was acting like cleaning up a ton of broken glass was right up there on her usual list of Saturday morning chores, alongside cleaning the toilets and getting groceries for the week. Barb looked like that type of parent, the kind that kept the house clean and bought trunk loads of groceries at a time, a week of meals mapped out on the fridge for easy reference.

"What happened?" Zoe asked. "Do you know who did this?"

Barb plunked Cassy back into the stroller. "Delinquents, ne'er-do-wells, hoodlums!" Barb tickled Cassy's belly, practically singing each word. "Drug addicts! Lunatics! Aliens!" She straightened. "I have no earthly idea, and the good Lord isn't giving any hints. My parents dropped us off this morning, and Bob's your uncle! Wait here."

Definitely suffering from shock, not the physiological kind, but the common deranged in-need-of-a-straightjacket kind. Not Dog, though. As soon as Barb deked inside, Dog put her hands on her hips.

"I bet you could tell me who did this, Zoe." She caught Zoe's nervous glance and held it like it belonged to her. "I bet you could, couldn't you?"

Zoe shook her head and turned the stroller in the other direction.

"You don't know?"

"No, I don't." Zoe pushed past Barb and her armload of musty yearbooks.

"Don't you want to see the pictures?"

"Another time, maybe." Zoe quickened her pace, getting away before she'd blurt out something she'd later regret, like the truth.

Earlier that week, Simon had told Zoe about Lisa Patterson. She'd been a Beckoner, although not for long. Last spring, just before the dog biscuit incident, the Beckoners had hacked off Lisa's hair with a pair of blunt scissors, then dry-shaved her head with a disposable razor and wrote "traitor" all over her nicked scalp and her face in indelible ink after she started dating some guy who'd dumped Heather back in grade eight. Zoe was not going to tell Dog or Barb or anybody that it was the Beckoners who smashed their windows. She still ate her lunch with them at the table in the smoke hole each day, because over the last week and a half that had become an expectation. She wasn't quite sure how she ended up there, and she was definitely not sure how she'd get herself out.

knife

Zoe had seen millions of movies in her life, not just because of her job at the theatre in Prince George, and not just because she was more intimate with her VCR than she was with most humans, but because she loved movies and planned to become rich and famous making them when she was finished with the depressing chore of being a minor.

Hanging out with the Beckoners was like being in a movie, and not a very good one either. Zoe swore the Beckoners lifted some of their bullshit straight from the movies, like that one evening at dusk, when they bombed down a narrow country road lined with farms, taking turns bashing mailboxes with a baseball bat. She was sure she'd seen that in at least two movies, although she couldn't recall which ones, so they couldn't have been very good.

Then there was the Tuesday they went to the movies, all of them sitting in the middle row, halfway to the front, draping their legs over the seats in front of them so no one could sit there.

A father and son, the son was maybe twelve, wanted the seats Beck's and Janika's feet were on. When they ignored the dad's protests and wouldn't move their feet, the dad sent the son to get an usher and glowered at them until the usher came.

"You can't have your feet on the chairs in front," the skinny acne victim mumbled without much conviction.

Beck saluted him and smiled. "Randall, how nice to see you still work here. That must mean our arrangement is working. Let's keep it that way."

"You're threatening him?" the dad fumed. "This is ridiculous!"

Zoe took her feet off the chair as he raised his voice, but Lindsay glared at her, so she put them back. Poor Randall.

Beck grinned at Randall.

"Look, sir, please," he begged the father, "I'll give you a coupon for two free movies and popcorn and drinks if you find somewhere else to sit."

"I'd take it," Janika said. "It's a good deal. If you sit in front of us our feet will be on your shoulders."

Jazz held up a large bag of popcorn. "And this will hit you, piece by annoying piece."

"Come on, Dad." The son pulled on his arm. "Let's sit somewhere else."

"I can't believe you get away with this." The dad took the coupons and shoved them in his pocket. "If you were my kids I'd be ashamed of you."

"Enjoy the movie, sir," Randall mumbled after them before slouching away up the aisle.

"Yeah," hollered Lindsay. "Enjoy the movie, asshole!"

The father turned and flashed her the finger.

"Shut up, Lindsay," Janika, Jazz, Heather and Beck all said at once.

Beck said to Zoe, "Our Lindsay never knows when enough is enough."

It was the stupidest movie Zoe had ever seen. It was a brainless, formulaic action film with re-hashed car chases, exploding buildings and dry, wooden dialogue. Zoe spent most of the movie laughing at how bad it was.

"It wasn't a comedy," Heather informed her when the lights came up. "It would've been nice if you'd shut up for five minutes."

That was the first time Heather had spoken to Zoe directly since that first day in the smoke hole.

"Oh, hi." Zoe held out her hand. "I'm Zoe. I don't think we've met."

"You think you're being cute?" Heather pushed past her and headed up the aisle. Beck and the others glared at Zoe.

"What?"

"Was that necessary?" Beck folded her arms. The group of them blocked the aisle, the people waiting to leave all watching.

"What? You want me to apologize? Fine. I'm sorry."

"Yeah?" Beck turned to leave. "Tell Heather that."

Zoe let the rest of the crowd leave ahead of her, half hoping the Beckoners would be gone by the time she got outside. She would not apologize to Heather. In the lobby, she debated leaving through the back, but if the Beckoners were waiting for her, they'd be pissed if she didn't show. Zoe pushed through the front doors, into the warm night.

She didn't have to apologize, not yet anyway. The Beckoners were waiting for her, in a rush to tail a shiny new Volvo out of the parking lot. The father from the theatre was driving, the son in the passenger seat, talking excitedly about something, hands flapping. Zoe squeezed in the front, along with Beck and Brady and his best friend Trevor. She avoided looking at

Heather, who was sitting on Lindsay's lap in the back seat of the big white truck.

They tailed the Volvo to a donut shop a couple of blocks away, where the father and son pulled in and parked. Brady waited on the street until the two of them disappeared inside, and then he turned off the stereo and rolled the truck to a stop behind the Volvo, so no one could see it from inside the donut shop.

Beck pulled a jackknife out of her pocket. It was a large old knife, the blade at least four inches long and shiny from a recent sharpening. Beck handed it to Zoe while she climbed over her to get out. Zoe was surprised at how heavy it was, how the smooth bone handle fit in her hand.

"My knife?" Beck waited, hand open.

"What are you going to do with it?"

"God," Heather said from the back. "Who *is* she?"

"Just give me the knife."

"But what are you—"

Beck grabbed the knife. "Thank you."

She walked around the Volvo, stabbing the four tires two or three times each, the Beckoners cheering her on.

Zoe was surprised at how slowly the air leaked out; it wasn't like the movies at all. When Beck was done, she dragged the knife blade across the paint, gouging a jagged line all around the car. When she was finished, she curtsied. The Beckoners gave her a hearty round of applause.

"What did you do that for?" Zoe blurted as Beck climbed back in the truck.

"If you have to ask, maybe we should drop you off at Rejoice In His Name." Beck wiped the paint flecks off her knife with the sleeve of her shirt as Brady screeched out of the lot. "Youth for Jesus do their talking in tongues or whatever there on Tuesday nights." Beck released the lock on the knife and folded it closed. Closed, the handle was nearly as long as her hand was wide.

"I was just asking," Zoe said. "It's no big deal."

"So then why ask?"

"No reason."

"Good."

"Fine."

"She's asking because she's a lame-ass wuss." Heather leaned forward, her face so close to Zoe's, Zoe could see the glitter in her eye shadow as they passed beneath a streetlight. "Isn't that right?"

"Whatever, Heather."

"You know what?" Beck frowned at Zoe and Heather. "The two of you would get along better if you both just shut the fuck up."

Zoe could handle that. When it came to Heather, she'd like nothing better than to never speak to her at all. In fact, she'd love to apply the same rule to all the Beckoners, but Beck had something else in mind, because no matter how hard Zoe tried to avoid her, Beck found her and dragged her along with the Beckoners on their lame movie cliché field trips. The only good thing about it was how much it pissed off Heather. Zoe thought that might become her new hobby: pissing off Heather.

That night, as they cruised through town on some pointless mission to find a guy who'd ripped off Trevor in a pot deal, they passed Dog and Shadow walking back to Paradise Heights from the corner store. Brady steered the truck across the road towards her, forcing a car in the other lane to swerve to avoid a head-on. He drove the truck right up onto the sidewalk, catching Dog in the headlights as she leapt out of the way and ran for it. Shadow froze and barked madly at the truck.

"Run him over!" Beck slapped the dash. "Come on, Brady. I dare you!"

"Don't!" Zoe reached across and grabbed the wheel.

"Shadow!" Dog screamed. "Come on, boy! COME HERE!"

Shadow barked once more at the truck and then crossed the road to Dog.

"*Don't!*" Heather mimicked Zoe's panic, which started them all laughing, except Zoe. "Like he would've, spaz case."

stuck

Mrs. Henley kept Zoe and Dog after class one day a couple of weeks later. Beck had skipped again, but Lindsay and Jazz were there to make it all worse than it had to be. They lingered after Mrs. Henley stepped out to fetch something from the office. They circled Dog's desk, howling quietly.

"Ugh, smells like wet dog." Lindsay scrunched up her nose. "Watch yourself, Zoe, you get any closer and you'll start reeking of it too. I think Dog should move her pimply ass."

Dog kept her eyes on Zoe.

"Move it!" Lindsay pointed to a desk in the very back corner.

Still, Dog stared, waiting for Zoe to prove she wasn't like the Beckoners.

Zoe could only think of Lisa Patterson, her scraped bald head and the words that wouldn't wash off.

"What are you looking at me for?" The words were pointed, but Zoe hoped her tone might soften them a little.

"You think Zoe gives a shit what I do to you?" Lindsay leaned over so she was looking straight down at Dog's dandruffy head. "You think anyone does?"

Jazz grabbed Dog's ears and made her shake her head.

"Zoe? Do you give a shit what I do to Dog?"

Zoe could barely hear her for the gusty winds battering her at the top of a perilous peak, cliffs dropping off on either side. At the bottom of one was the cruel backstabbing place the Beckoners infested, a place crawling with nasty-ass comebacks and vindictive she-devils. At the bottom of the other was the equally terrible wasteland of the bullied. If she said yes, she'd fall there, and while they were both horrible, one was certainly safer than the other.

"No," Zoe said miserably, looking at her feet.

Dog looked away when Zoe said that. Even after the first dig, she'd been willing to give Zoe another chance, she wasn't a real Beckoner, not yet, but there she was sinking deeper into that bitch place, that pick-on-the-little-guy place, that ugly and competitive bullying place.

In one of his "Simon Says" moments, Simon had told Zoe about the day of the fire alarm, the day the Beckoners made Dog eat all those dog biscuits. Now Zoe understood why Simon hadn't done anything to stop them, why no one had. It was all about survival. Everyone had to look out for themselves. Dog was just really really bad at it.

When Mrs. Henley came back, she surveyed the scene: Zoe, Lindsay and Jazz at the front, heads together, and Dog, scribbling in her notebook, exiled at the back of the room. She told Lindsay and Jazz to leave, and asked Dog to come back up to the front. Mrs. Henley leaned against the desk, arms folded, looking down her nose at the unlikely pair.

"Should I ask what that was about?"

Dog shook her head. At least she knew that much about survival.

"No?"

Dog shook her head again.

Mrs. Henley looked at Zoe. She shook her head too. "Okay then, on to business. I've had the delight of looking over your records from Prince George, Zoe. You and April should both be in Advanced English, and I apologize on behalf of this overdrawn school district for not having the resources to make that a reality at this point. However, I offer you this. I will give you extra assignments, and in the end, you'll be credited for Advanced English."

Dog looked at Zoe, a big dumb grin on her face, like all of a sudden, never mind all that crap before, she'd been awarded a new best friend. Friends by default. In that way, she really was a dog; kick it one second and call it the next, and it'll race back, tongue lolling happily. "Thanks, Mrs. H!"

Mrs. Henley smiled at Dog. "And how does that arrangement work for you, Miz Anderson?"

"Will we have to leave class to do the extra work?" Zoe imagined long hours in the library, stuck with Dog.

Mrs. Henley shook her head. "You'll work on them in class, and on your own time. Does that suit you?"

"Yeah."

"You mean to say 'yes.'"

"Yes. Thanks."

"Why do I get the impression that this is bothersome to you?"

"No, it's not. It's fine."

"Fine?" Mrs. Henley glanced at the papers in her hand. "Why don't I believe you? Would you like to let me in on why this is problematic for you? Does it have anything to do with Lindsay and Jazz?"

Dog swallowed hard, waiting for Zoe to spit it out that she'd rather stick with the regular curriculum than spend time with her and get extra credit.

Mrs. Henley waited for her answer, but Zoe didn't know what to say. "I'll assume your silence indicates that this arrangement will work for you." She handed them each a notice with the school paper's letterhead at the top. "These are the rules for the essay contest. Your first extra assignment is to enter it. That will be all. You may leave."

On the way out, Dog whispered to Zoe, like there was anyone to hear, "The winner gets to be the assistant editor for the whole year, you know."

Didn't she get it? Do. Not. Talk. To. Zoe. Zoe would've said that, but Mrs. Henley was at the door watching them leave.

"Wow. Really."

Dog couldn't even take the hint of Zoe's flat, sarcastic response. On the contrary, she accepted Zoe's words as a free-for-all to let her rip. "Yeah, you get your own desk, in the Dungeon—that's the newspaper room—and you get to have a by-line on anything you write. And the editor is totally—"

Lindsay and Jazz were waiting at the stairs. That shut her up. She stopped in her tracks, jaw slack.

"What's the matter?" Lindsay faked a lunge at her. Dog reeled back, as if Lindsay had hit her for real. "Are you afwaid of wittle ole me?"

Dog turned and ran in the other direction, Lindsay and Jazz barking after her until Mrs. Henley popped her head out of the room.

"I suggest the three of you find somewhere else to behave like preschoolers."

Lindsay and Jazz pretended not to hear. They went ahead, still barking, but not so loud.

"Yes, ma'am." Zoe kept her eyes down as she passed.

"Zoe?" Mrs. Henley stepped into the hall, hands on her hips.

"Yes, Mrs. Henley?"

"I expect more from you."

Zoe didn't know what to say in reply, so she just nodded and stood there until Mrs. Henley went back into the room and shut the door.

initiation

Zoe had no idea it was coming. One night, Lindsay showed up at her door and escorted her, silently, down the driveway to Brady's truck. Nobody said a word, all the way to Mill Lake. Janika stayed behind with her at the truck while the rest of them went ahead, and then Janika walked her across the field towards the bandstand, where the rest of the Beckoners were waiting, still silent.

"I was scared too," Janika whispered when they were halfway across the damp grass.

"I'm not scared."

"Liar."

"Okay, I'm scared. Is it a dare?"

"No questions, Zoe."

"Tell me if it's going to hurt, Janika. That's not a question."

Janika shook her head and sped up, walking ahead of Zoe, like she was supposed to be doing in the first place.

In a corner of the bandstand, Brady held a fork over the flame of a small butane torch. The end was wrapped thick with masking tape, so it wouldn't get too hot to hold. Zoe took one look at that and knew it was going to hurt. The others stood in a tight circle until Beck nodded; then they stepped aside and Janika led Zoe into the middle.

Beck stepped forward. "You will not speak, understood?"

Zoe nodded.

"Roll up your sleeve," Beck instructed. "Up to your shoulder."

Zoe took off her jacket and pushed up her left sleeve.

"No, your right one. We all have it on the right arm."

Zoe rolled up her other sleeve. What on the right arm?

"Arm out, palm up. Lindsay will hold you steady."

The fork glowed a fierce orange. Beck took off her jacket and pushed up her own sleeve. On the fleshy inside of her arm, just below her shoulder, were four raised scars, lined up like the prongs of a fork. "This is the Beckoner mark."

Zoe sucked in her breath.

"Rule number one." Heather stepped into the circle, grinning. "No speaking, at all, unless we give you permission." Zoe saw Beck frown. "Unless Beck gives you permission, I mean. Rule number two: keep your eyes open." Heather sounded happier than Zoe had ever heard her, yet she couldn't want this. This was going to make Zoe a real Beckoner. This meant she was one of them, as much as Heather was. Surely, she didn't want that? "Rule number three: if you cry or yell or scream or even close your eyes, it's over. You don't get another chance. Rule number four: once it's done, there's no turning back. You're one of us, forever."

Suddenly, Zoe understood. That stuck-up prima donna thought Zoe couldn't hack it. She thought Zoe would chicken out. She thought Zoe would fail. There she was, ticking the rules off her fingers, all the while thinking Zoe couldn't handle it. Zoe narrowed her eyes at Heather.

"It's ready," Brady said, still holding the fork over the flame.

"Are you ready, Zoe?" Beck asked.

"You never asked me that," Heather said. "You never asked any of us that. Just get on with it. She's not going to make it, are you, Zoe? You're going to scream so loud someone's going to think you're being raped. So long, Zoe." She gave Zoe that little fake wave, that billboard-bitch wave that might as well be mechanized. "Been a splash, sweetie."

Bad move, Heather, Zoe thought. Don't ever tell Zoe that she can't do something. Don't tell her how she's going to react. Don't presume to know her, when you don't. Don't think for one nasty little slice of a second that you're so almighty you've got her figured out. Go home, Heather, and rot in your palatial princess suite, with its antique sleigh bed and in-floor heating and dedicated phone line. Zoe forgot all her doubts about being associated with the Beckoners. In that moment, she just wanted to prove Heather wrong.

"I'm ready."

"So what, now we do it when she says so?" Heather looked to the others for support. "We need her permission?"

"Shut up, Heather." Beck didn't look at her. "I decide when I do it."

"Great, glad to know there's still some element of surprise."

"Shut up, Heather."

"Fuck you, Beck. Tell me to shut up one more time and I'm leaving."

There was a silence, carefully loaded by Beck, a long pause that made it clear that Beck was thinking that might not be such a bad idea. Heather folded her arms and stepped back into the circle. Zoe had to fight back a smile.

Zoe stood in the middle of the circle, shivering. She tried to stop by taking deep breaths, but that didn't work. She looked at the floor instead, trying to see past the wood slats, to the ground below. She imagined being there, huddled in the damp dark, looking up at this scene. She imagined she was not this person who was about to be branded.

Then a sour stench hit her nose like a full-force fist. Pain sliced through her as if she was being cut in half by it. Lindsay was holding her shoulders so tight Zoe couldn't move, even if she had wanted to bolt. She clamped her free hand over her mouth and bit down hard on the fleshy skin below her thumb. She opened her eyes as wide as they'd go and stared up at the starless sky, slivers of smoke slipping into sight. That was her skin, burning, the smoke shifting into the atmosphere, particles of her joining the universe. Beck watched her face while the others counted.

"One, one thousand, two, one thousand..."

Silently, Zoe named the constellations she couldn't see: Ursa Major, Big Dipper...Orion...Andromeda. She couldn't think of any more. They tumbled around in her head with the same chaotic velocity as her heartbeat. Then Beck lifted the fork away and it was over.

Zoe was one of them. She was a Beckoner. She meant to look at her arm right away, but she looked for Heather instead, who was halfway to the parking lot, swearing like a drunk. Janika hurried after her, calling for her to wait up.

The only thing Zoe could compare it to is when she got her first period.

She and Alice had been camping in the Rockies, the summer Alice was massively pregnant with Cassy. They were in the provincial campground, surrounded by convoys of German tourists in rental campers. After a week of trading English swearwords for German ones, Zoe woke up sticky and damp between her legs. She knew what had happened. The same thing that landed Alice on the couch three days every month, clutching the hot water bottle to her belly, talk shows turned low so they wouldn't make her headaches worse. She moaned and groaned, but through it all insisted that your monthly was Mother Nature's way of announcing your womanhood and it was nothing to be ashamed or afraid of, no matter how excruciating your cramps might be, or what a bitch you were the week before.

After Alice gushed all over her, grabbing her cheeks in her hands and blinking back tears as she soaked Zoe's face with kisses, they left to drive into Banff to get the sleeping bag cleaned and to buy tampons. Zoe made Alice pull into the first gas station on the highway so she could get a good look at herself in a decent mirror. There were three people ahead of her in line for the bathroom. While she waited, she braced herself for the new Zoe. She was a woman now. Yesterday, she hadn't been. She would have to expect to look completely different, right?

When it was her turn at last she stood in front of the mirror and wept. She looked exactly the same, only dirtier and pimplier after a week of camping.

That's how she felt the morning after the initiation. She looked exactly the same as the day before, except now she also had a seeping wound she'd been ordered not to doctor, because it scarred better if she didn't put anything on it.

alice

Zoe didn't see her mother the night of the initiation. She didn't see her all the next day, either, which was a Sunday. Zoe woke to find Cassy asleep beside her, on her belly, diapered bum sticking up, fists under her chin. A note on the fridge thanked Zoe for looking after Cassy for the day. Zoe had not been informed that that was what she was doing with her day, and while she was mad at Alice for presuming that she'd have nothing better to do, she was thankful for an excuse to stay home and hide from the Beckoners. Zoe packed Cassy into the stroller and walked to the video store for a load of movies, which she watched one after the other while Cassy carefully and repeatedly dumped out and refilled her dinosaur cup with grapes.

"Eat them, bratscicle," Zoe said when the grapes started to get slimy.

Cassy shook her head.

And that was the extent of their conversation for the day.

She finally saw Alice on Sunday night, but if Alice noticed anything different about Zoe, like how she favored the arm with the scar, or how she skulked around holding on to a secret, she didn't mention anything.

"When am I going to get paid for all this babysitting?" Zoe said when her mother walked in the front door.

"We all have to do our part, Zoe." Alice looked haggard, as if she'd had a long hard day at work. However, it was her day off, so it was more likely she'd found someone to party with. She smelled of the bar, although all the bars in Abbotsford were closed on Sundays.

"In other words, I'm never getting paid for it?" Zoe scooped Cassy away from her pile of blocks and started stuffing her into her jacket. "I'm donating my time so that you can go and party?" Zoe headed for the door, Cassy in tow.

"You know, you're lucky to have a roof over your head." Alice sunk onto the couch, her coat bunching up to her shoulders. "Maybe you should come donate some of your precious time at Fraser House, so you don't go losing perspective on how good you got it, a roof over your head and food in the cupboards. That's a hell of a lot more than some, you know."

"You had a look at the cupboards lately?" Zoe took down four boxes of macaroni and cheese, a half empty box of soda crackers and three chicken noodle soup mixes. "That's all there is."

Alice held up a finger. "Watch where you're going with that, missy." She closed her eyes and rested her head against the back of the couch.

It had to be a new man. Even Alice was pretty good about keeping food in the house. She might not be the kind of mother who was very organized about it, but she'd usually come home with a couple of bags every other night or so, and it had been almost a week since she'd done any shopping at all.

"Cassy and I'll go to the store." Zoe fished in her mother's purse for her wallet. Her hand landed on a letter. Zoe checked that Alice's eyes were still closed before she peeked at it. It was a love letter, written by someone who was trying hard to write neatly. The words sloped down to the right, "Sweetheart, Even the thought of your firm…"

"Get the hell out of my purse!" Alice cleared the space between the couch and the table in two steps. "What the hell you digging in there for?"

"Money! For food?"

"Well, Jesus, Zoe, don't go snooping." Alice handed her a twenty and took her purse back to the couch with her. "Get me a pack of cigarettes out of that, would you?"

Zoe let Cassy walk the whole way to the store, which meant the trip took nearly an hour, rather than the fifteen minutes it would have if Zoe had gone on her own. Cassy stopped to look at everything that caught her eye. She collected pebbles, squatting down and dropping them into her dinosaur cup. Zoe walked behind her, wondering about this man, this love letter writer, this somebody who was thinking about Alice's firm whatever.

When she and Cassy got home, Alice was upstairs in her bedroom on the phone with the door shut. Her purse was on the couch. Zoe rifled through it, looking for the thick cream colored paper, but it was gone.

fallout

The pain of the branding was much worse on Monday. It had only really throbbed all day Sunday. That hadn't been so bad; but by mid-morning Monday, Zoe couldn't remember what it was like *not* to be in pain. It ached, it throbbed, it seemed to have developed its own voice and was now screaming in agony. The throbbing was a constant soft thud. When Zoe closed her eyes the thudding got louder. "Dumb, dumb, dumb," it seemed to pound in her head and Zoe couldn't disagree. She ducked into the handicapped bathroom between classes and locked the door. She looked at it in the mirror. It was festering, probably writhing in the clutches of some gross infection. Before she headed out, Zoe rinsed it with cold water, wincing back the tears.

Science was next. Just after Mr. Turner had taken off after attendance and most of the class was gone, Zoe showed Simon the scar and told him about Saturday night.

"You didn't!" Simon's lips curled in disgust at the sight of the wound. He lowered his voice so that the few others who'd stayed behind wouldn't hear. "You are in so deep. I don't think there's anything left for me to even *say*."

"But I had to—"

"I don't see any puppet strings."

"You don't understand."

"Don't give me that shit. I completely understand." Simon grabbed her wrist. "Come with me." He dragged her into the hallway. "Okay. I'm all ears. What the hell were you thinking?"

"I didn't get a chance to think." Zoe pulled her sleeve gingerly back over the wound. "It just kind of happened."

"Bullshit." He folded his arms and frowned. "You want this?"

Zoe shrugged. She'd just wanted to wipe that smile off of Heather's face, which she'd accomplished beautifully. She opened her mouth to say that, but then she decided she didn't want him to know that about her.

"You would've done the same thing if you were me, Simon."

He took an extra long drawn-out breath before answering. "Um, no, Zoe. I would not have done the same thing if I were you."

"What would you have done?"

"Told them in no uncertain terms to get that cow brand away from my perfect, blemish-free skin, thank you very much."

"Oh, sure. As if." Zoe wanted to tell him that would not have worked. She wanted to tell him that he had to be there to understand why she went through with it. He had to have seen the way Heather gloated. Zoe wanted to tell him about how Heather thought she couldn't do it. How she was just so bloody sure Zoe wouldn't go through with it. She wanted to tell him it was no different than Teo's Gemini tattoo at the base of his neck. She wanted to take his hands and make him stay there until he'd tell her he didn't think less of her.

The look on Simon's face made perfectly clear just how much less he thought of her. He turned on his heel and went back into the lab, leaving her out in the hallway feeling as if she'd lost her virginity to some loser she'd thought was cool when they were alone together, but in the light of day turned out to be a freak nobody else wanted to be in the same room with.

One thing didn't change after the initiation; Heather still acted as if Zoe did not exist. Well, even that did change a little; before, Heather had looked right through Zoe. Now, she didn't even bother doing that. If they were anywhere near each other, Heather ever so slightly turned her face away in a carefully executed gesture of dismissal. Lindsay, Janika and Jazz didn't know how to act.

"It's kind of weird," Janika confided in her when they were alone together in gym. "We don't really bring in new people. Or, we did once, but she didn't really work out."

Zoe figured Lisa Patterson would put it a little more emphatically than that.

"Well, I didn't ask for it, did I?"

"You don't want to be a Beckoner?"

"I didn't say that either."

"But you're acting like it."

"It's just Heather..." Zoe wasn't sure how to end the statement. She kicked at a basketball that had escaped in their direction. "She doesn't—she's just so bitchy."

"But there's the rest of us," Janika said. "It's not all Heather. Heather's just extra pissed off because of what happened at the park."

"Is she ever going to be finished being pissed off?"

Janika shrugged as the gym teacher whistled for her to get into the game.

"She's been pissed off as long as I've known her."

Then why be her friend at all? Zoe watched Janika snatch the ball from another girl and make a basket from halfway down the court.

Simon started talking to Zoe again towards the end of the week.

"I've been thinking," he said as a greeting. "Come with me." He hooked her arm with his and pulled her towards the ravine.

Teo came along, until the three of them reached the trail that lead down into the ravine.

"Aren't you coming?" Zoe called behind her as Simon pulled her down the trail.

"I've been instructed to keep watch for the Beckoners," Teo said.

Zoe let Simon drag her all the way down to the bottom of the ravine. It wasn't likely that the Beckoners would surface any time soon. They'd gone in Janika's sister's car to hotbox at Mill Lake. As far as Zoe knew, they weren't going to be back all afternoon. Zoe had managed to get out of that little escapade. There was no way she could miss her lab quiz that afternoon. She was sure that at some point, probably pretty soon, Beck would stop buying the excuses Zoe made up to get out of going with them.

Simon led Zoe to the little clearing where he and Teo hung out when they skipped class.

"Sit." He pointed to one of the lawn chairs drawn up to an old cable spool table. Zoe sat. Simon paced.

"Am I in for a 'Simon Says' moment?" From her sitting postition, Zoe thought Simon looked even taller than he really was. Zoe grinned. "Bring it on. I can take it."

Simon stopped. "This isn't funny."

Zoe removed her grin. "Sorry."

"This is not some joke, Zoe." Simon sat in the other chair. "I've been thinking really hard about whether or not to tell you this."

Zoe's heart started pounding in anticipation. "Tell me what?"

"You know my verbal seizures, as Teo puts them, what I call essential thoughts and information on important subjects?"

Zoe nodded.

"I had to think about whether or not what I'm about to tell you falls in that category. I always kept it a secret. When I promise to keep a secret, I keep it."

"Then don't tell me." Zoe was pretty sure she didn't want to know, judging by Simon's conflicted expression.

"I've decided I'm going to."

"Maybe you shouldn't?"

"I am." Simon placed his hands on his knees. "I am going to tell you."

"Whose secret is it?"

"Beck's!" Simon rolled his eyes. "Of course it's about Beck. Isn't everything about Beck?"

"No."

"Well, this is." He put a hand to his stomach. "Feels weird breaking a promise."

"Then don't tell me!"

"It's not about not telling you anymore." Simon placed his other hand on his stomach too. "It's about me feeling guilty that I didn't tell you sooner, but I didn't know they were going to initiate you. If I had known, I would've told you. I know I would've."

"Now you have to tell me because you're scaring me."

Simon took a deep breath.

"We were eleven. Beginning of grade six. Beck was making scrambled eggs in one of those iron skillets. You know those really heavy ones?"

Zoe nodded.

"She was making her dad breakfast. She always made his breakfast. He worked nights and was just coming home. So I guess it wouldn't really be his breakfast, because he went to bed right after. I remember going over there to play and we had to talk in whispers because her dad was sleeping. He was always really grumpy—" Simon stopped talking as Zoe cocked her head at him, a gesture to stick to the topic.

"Anyway, the phone rang and she answered it and it was Heather and they started talking and the eggs started burning. Mr. Wilson came in just as the smoke alarm went off. He went off too. He grabbed her and he grabbed the fork she'd left in the hot pan and he burnt her with it." Simon pointed on his own arm, the same spot Zoe had her scar. "Branded her."

Zoe swallowed. "How do you know that's what happened?"

"We used to walk to school together. I came to the door just after. The smoke alarm was still screaming. So was Beck. I ran home and told my mom. She phoned the police. I remember she let me stay home from school that day."

"What about Beck?"

"She went and stayed at Heather's for a few days. A social worker checked up on them after that, or that's what they told my mom would happen anyway. I don't really know."

"The Beckoners?" Zoe stared at her lap. "When did that start?"

"Heather did it right away. And then the others, one a year on the anniversary until they all had it and there was no one else. So last year they tried Lisa Patterson. And now you."

"Why me?" Zoe looked up.

Simon shrugged. "The five of them have always been best friends. There's no one left, unless they were going to start doing matching ones on the other arm. I don't know why Beck wants to keep doing it."

"How long did Lisa Patterson last?"

Simon shrugged again. "Not long."

Zoe felt sick while she was writing her lab quiz that afternoon. The pulsing pain in her arm was worse: dumb, dumb, dumb, dumb.

Mr. Turner collected the quizzes and then redistributed them for the students to mark each other. Simon got Zoe's. She'd failed, but Simon erased her wrong answers and circled the correct ones so that she aced it in the end, or it looked like that anyway.

leaf

Simon made Zoe promise never to tell Beck what he'd told her in the ravine. It was a double cross-my-heart, hope-to-die, curse-me-if-I-don't kind of promise. Zoe felt a little sorry for Beck now. She was at Beck's house one night, waiting for her in the living room with the others while she was still upstairs in the shower. Mr. Wilson was getting ready to go to work. Mrs. Wilson padded around the kitchen, putting his lunch together, the bottom of her long sweater flapping against her pale veiny calves. Mr. Wilson grumbled about his coveralls not being dry, the car needing gas, his lunch not being ready and his cigarettes being lost. When he left, Mrs. Wilson perked up considerably.

"Do you kids want some hot chocolate?" She kept her ear directed at the door, listening to the car back down the drive. She wore too much makeup. When she smiled, her eyebrows were dark arches over blue eye shadow ponds. Zoe wanted to wet a facecloth and wipe it off. She wanted to sit Mrs. Wilson down in a chair and bring *her* a mug of hot chocolate.

Zoe had not expected to feel sorry for Beck. It made backing away a little more difficult, because now there was the added complication of having empathy for the very person she was trying to extricate herself from. Before Simon told her about Beck's dad, Zoe's first move was going to be to tell the Beckoners about Mrs. Henley putting her and Dog together in the Mrs. Henley's Underground Program for Gifted Children. It's not that Zoe still didn't think that was a good place to start. She wanted Beck to know she was choosing to stay in it, even though Dog was the only other student. She wanted Beck to know that she cared about other things, that she was interested in other things, that she was more than someone with Beck's warped idea of an initiation scar on her arm.

But so far, Zoe hadn't told her about Mrs. Henley. She was going to; in fact, one morning she decided she was going to tell her after class, but then in came Mrs. Henley waving a copy of the school paper. The essay contest. Zoe had started and finished her entry the day it was due and hadn't given it another thought until this moment. She hoped Mrs. Henley wouldn't say anything about it that would link her with Dog.

"Seats, everyone! I have the winning essay in hand. The author of which, as you all know, will be the assistant editor at the *Central Reporter* this year."

A couple of kids in the front row leaned forward, trying to read the name at the top. Mrs. Henley wagged a finger at them.

"I don't think so. We have a special guest coming to announce the winner. By now you've all probably guessed, unless you are in fact cretins, that the winner is a member of this very class. Beck, eyes to the front. You and Lindsay can plot your overthrow of the government later, I'm sure."

"Just tell us who it is," Beck said. "No one cares anyway."

"Well, Beck—" Mrs. Henley was interrupted by a knock at the door. In walked a wiry guy with rock star yellow-tinted glasses, black hair with blue tips hanging in his face, cuffs of his black jeans folded up, a dark gray work shirt undone over a black Ramones T-shirt, a stack of the school paper under one arm and a vintage *Dick Tracy* lunchbox in the other hand.

"As I was about to say, Beck, I can think of at least one other person who cares besides myself." Mrs. Henley waved him in. "Our esteemed editor himself, Leaf Morrison."

In that instant, Zoe became fairly sure she was not a lesbian.

"Hey." Leaf nodded at the class.

His voice was deep, midnight radio announcer smooth. Zoe hadn't thought that teenaged boys could sound that cool.

Mrs. Henley beamed at him. "For those of you who don't know, Leaf is in his last year here at Central and has been the editor for the past two years. Leaf, the honor is yours. Don't keep us in suspense, child."

"This lunchbox is filled with everything an assistant editor needs to do the job." Leaf set the lunchbox on Mrs. Henley's desk. "It's been passed down from assistant editor to assistant editor since 1958. It's got your standard pens, pencils, notebooks, instant coffee and cigarettes." The class laughed. "There are some modern conveniences as well, a mini disc recorder and a photocopier key. This year it goes to—" he checked the name, "—April Donelly for her essay about teenage mothers at Central, running front page in this issue, hot off the press." He thumped the stack of papers. "Congratulations, April. April?"

The class was silent.

"Which one's April?"

"This is a joke, right?" Beck laughed. "You're not serious."

Leaf turned to Mrs. Henley. "Is she here, Mrs. H?"

"April!" Mrs. Henley waved the paper at Dog. "You won! Stand up, say a few words, child. Congratulations!"

"Um." Dog pushed herself up in her seat just a bit. "Um, thanks."

Leaf's expression changed from curious anticipation to sinking dread and back in less than five seconds. A very quick recovery. "Hi. April. Donelly. Right."

"Look at him, he had no idea it was Dog!" Beck laughed again.

"Beck, I've asked you before not to—"

"You absolutely have to pick someone else, Henley. She's not mentally fit for the job. Aren't I right, Lindsay?"

"A complete nutcase."

"Jazz? Back me up here."

"Big mistake, Mrs. H."

"Enough! If you'd bothered to notice, the winner was selected by blind judging. I trust you all at least know what that means?" There was a definite edge to Mrs. Henley's voice. "So, it has already been proven that she has the skill. If you have such a vested interest, I suggest you enter the contest next year. April? Are you all right?"

Dog stared at her desktop. She'd watched Leaf's penny drop, followed immediately by his quick scramble to pick it up. The whole class had seen it.

"She's always like that," Beck said.

"Zombie," Lindsay said. "Completely brain dead. She should be institutionalized. It's very sad."

"The two of you, that is more than enough! April, why don't you take this opportunity to check out the Dungeon with Leaf? I believe there's a desk there with your name on it. Leaf?"

"Yeah. Right. There is." Leaf studied Dog as she got her books together, his brow furrowing. Dog scurried to the front of the room, taking a circuitous route up an aisle well out of reach of Beck.

If only Zoe had spent more time on her essay. And why had she picked such a stupid topic? Nobody cared if there was no main entrée for vegetarians in the school café. Vegetarians were pathetic anemic losers, Zoe decided as she watched Dog leave, and she, Zoe Anderson was a complete and total idiot.

"There goes the paper," Beck said as Dog left without so much as shaking Leaf's reluctantly stuck out hand as she passed. He dropped his hand and looked at Mrs. Henley, who was proudly passing a newspaper to each student. The look he laid on her was one of abject disappointment, as though she'd duped him on purpose, as though she should've known better than to let this happen. He stared at her back, and then collected the lunchbox and left the room without another word.

By lunchtime that day, the school was barking at Dog with a renewed enthusiasm. Simon and Teo and Zoe walked behind her down the hall as Dog headed out of the school. Dog looked like she wanted to bolt, but was resisting. Zoe had to give her credit. If she bolted, it proved they'd gotten to her. Ignoring it was a small triumph that at least suggested that she didn't care. The barking stopped when Dog stepped outside, because of course all the barkers would look pretty stupid if there were no Dog to bark at.

"That girl is so marked." Simon said as the door slowly shut behind her. "You'd think the air around her would be a different color."

Zoe stopped at her locker to grab her lunch, and then the three of them went outside. There was Dog, whistling to Shadow, who'd been waiting at the curb across the street. He bounded over to her as best he could with his stiff legs. Zoe and the boys watched Dog make her way down the path between the portables to the little strip of grass she ate her lunch on, alone with her dog, every day.

If Zoe had Mrs. Henley's job, she would've taken Dog's essay out of the running. She would've slipped it out of the pile and tucked it in her satchel and fed it to the fireplace at home, because even if she was a hoity-toity English teacher at the sunset end of a fifty-year generation gap, Zoe would've known better than to keep Dog in the running. Never, ever, ever focus the spotlight on someone who is naked and alone and tiny in the world.

Simon and Teo went on ahead while Zoe watched Dog take her lunch out of a paper bag and line it up in front of her on the grass: apple, cheese sandwich on brown bread, juice box, granola bar, carrot sticks in a baggie. She gave Shadow half the sandwich, looking up to see if anyone was watching. Zoe ducked. Squatting there just outside the main doors with students passing, wiping the strange looks off their faces when they realized it was a Beckoner hiding there like she was about to take a dump in the bushes, Zoe discovered she was actually a little jealous of Dog. Zoe had to admit she'd rather be Dog, sharing a quiet, private patch of grass with Shadow instead of looking forward to yet another lunch hour in the smoke hole, fending off Heather's psychic vampirism and the general inanity of the Beckoners.

happy birthday

The night of Beck's sixteenth birthday changed everything.

Zoe wasn't going to go. She didn't want to, and it was at Heather's, so she'd assumed that even if Beck wanted her there, Heather wouldn't let her through the front door.

"What the hell do you think?" Beck had said when Zoe told her she wasn't going. "You're a Beckoner. You go. Don't be an idiot."

Alice was covering an overnight shift at the shelter, so she'd arranged for the young mom who lived next door to babysit Cassy. Her name was Wish. Zoe expected a willowy hippie girl with messy dreads and flowing skirts and moccasins and silver bangles on her wrists, the kind of mom who breastfed her kid until they were four. Wish showed up half an hour before she was supposed to, and she was no hippie.

Standing there, clutching a squalling, writhing toddler in her arms, was the most pierced person Zoe had ever seen. In addition to the small thick rings lining her ears, she had metal in her nose, lower lip, both eyebrows, and in the space between her eyes, which was hard to see above her silver-rimmed, rhinestoned cat's-eye glasses.

"Zoe?" She shifted the kid to her hip and held out her hand. "I'm Wish, hi."

"You're early." Zoe tried not to stare at the stud in her tongue.

"Yeah, uh…look, I've got to take Connor to Emergency." She put her palm to his brow. "He's got a massive temperature. I'm really sorry."

"Don't worry about it." Zoe was relieved to have an excuse not to go, an excuse even Beck had to buy. "I'll stay home, it's no big deal."

"Oh, you can still go. Mrs. D's daughter is coming. I called your mom. She said that was okay."

"Really?" Zoe hesitated. "She said it was okay? You're sure?"

"Yeah, I'm sure. You can call her if you want, but she said it was no problem. Make it quick though, because I got to go."

"No, no. That's okay." Zoe watched a black tow-truck with silver lettering on the side pull in, its diesel engine idling, thrasher music pulsing from the cab. Wish pushed a chunk of purple hair out of her eyes and waved at the driver. From the doorway all Zoe could see of him was that he had freaky black hair and a huge bullring through his nose.

"That's T-Bone. I have to go."

When the doorbell rang half an hour later, it was Dog standing there, dressed in saggy-kneed overalls, notebook sticking out of her pocket. Shadow sat at her feet, tail wagging.

"What are *you* doing here?"

"I thought you were out." Dog's words were just as sharp as Zoe's. "I thought your mom was here."

"She's at work. You're Mrs. D's daughter, of course." Zoe smacked her forehead. "Mrs. *Donelly.* I thought everyone called her Barb."

"You didn't know it was me?"

"No, I didn't."

"I'll go." She gestured back towards her house. "I'll just go."

"No, no. I was just surprised, that's all." Zoe checked both ways, just in case Janika was on her way. "Come in." Janika was supposed to pick her up and Zoe did not want her to see Dog being ushered into her house. But here was a perfect opportunity to show Dog that she wasn't like the others. "Come on in."

"You're sure the coast is clear?" April said sarcastically.

"I was just seeing if my ride was here."

"Uh-huh," April said. "Can Shadow come in? I won't babysit for you unless he can come in."

"Whatever, sure." Zoe checked the road again. No Janika yet. "Just come in."

Shadow trotted in happily, turned around in circles by the couch and plunked himself down under the coffee table, grizzled chin on his big paws.

"He won't make a mess or anything."

"Whatever. It's fine with me, really." Zoe gave her a quick tour of the place, apologizing for the lack of junk food and the fact that they only had two channels.

Janika hollered from out front. Zoe stiffened. She stepped in front of Dog, so Janika wouldn't see her right away if she barged in.

"Uh, I don't know when I'll be home." Zoe pulled on her jacket and backed towards the door. "Is that okay?"

"It doesn't matter. It's not like I have plans or anything."

Janika pounded on the kitchen window, her dark saucer eyes peeking in. Zoe waved at her and she disappeared. Zoe hesitated at the door. Dog stood there, hands stuffed into her pockets.

"Well, thanks," Zoe said. "For doing this on such short notice and everything."

Dog shrugged. "I wasn't doing anything anyway."

"Still, thanks—" Zoe was just about to call her Dog to her face, but she caught herself. "Thanks, April."

At Heather's, Lindsay flung open the front door. "Janika! Girlfriend!" she slurred. "Get your skinny black ass in here!" She smelled of beer and of her musky perfume, which she'd put too much of on, as usual. She pointed her drink at Zoe and practically hollered, "You brought *her*! Man, Heather's going to freak!"

Zoe watched the taxi pull away, brake lights disappearing around the curve. She was stranded.

Zoe wandered through the crowded house and found Beck in the kitchen, sitting cross-legged on an island counter in the middle of the room. Heather stood in front of her, leaning against Beck's legs. Brady was in front of Heather, his hands gripping her hips. Zoe stood in the doorway for a while, watching Beck. People bee-lined to her, bringing her drinks and birthday gifts. She had a red feather boa draped around her neck, and a tight black T-shirt with the words *sugar & spice* on it in curvy silver letters across her chest. She evaluated each of the gifts when the giver left the room, either flinging it over her shoulder or adding it to the little pile beside her. She was tanked, her movements exaggerated and sloppy.

After a long while, she noticed Zoe. She winked slowly at her.

"Zooooooooooooe. What the hell kind of name is that, huh? Zoooe. Zzz, ooooh, eeeee." She kicked a red boot in her direction. It skidded onto the counter near her, sending a full whiskey bottle smashing to the floor. Everybody laughed except Heather.

"'What the hell is she doing here? I told you I didn't want her in my house, ever."

"It's my party, right?" Beck leaned into Heather's face. "And I want her here."

"You should've told me."

"You would've said no."

"Exactly." Heather pushed her away and scowled at Zoe.

Zoe picked up a dishtowel and bent to clean up the mess. Beck pushed herself off the counter, staggered over and grabbed her shirt.

"No, no, no. Slave boy will do that." She snapped her fingers. A boy, maybe ten years old, dressed in a sheet draped like a toga leapt to attention from where he'd been washing wineglasses at the sink. "Clean it up, slave boy."

He curled his lip at Beck and turned back to the sink.

"Move it, Malcolm!" Heather pointed a fake-nailed finger at him. "And I swear, you tell Mom, I'll pull your teeth out with pliers. You got that?"

Malcolm scurried towards the broken glass.

"I'll help him," Zoe said.

"Yeah," Heather said, "You do that, sweetie."

"No, no, no you don't," Beck said. "He's mine and I want him to do it all by himself and I want him to sing too. I want a singing slave boy. Sing something!"

Malcolm muttered something nobody could hear over the music.

"What?" Beck leaned forward, nearly toppling off the counter. "WHAT?"

"I don't know any songs."

"You do so." Beck squinted at him. "You have Mrs. Allan, right?"

He nodded.

"Then you know 'Michael Row Your Boat Ashore.' Sing that."

He shook his head.

"Sing it!" Heather chucked a plastic cup at his head. "Don't piss her off, Malcolm. She owns you. Do what she says."

Malcolm started singing, his voice a tiny little warble under the bass thump from the dining room.

Poor Malcolm. He kneeled in the pool of whiskey, ducking his head to hide the tears, his blue underwear peeking out from the folds of the sheet, singing his song over and over as he picked up the glass. He looked so pathetically embarrassed and wilted, Zoe wanted to steer him out of there and take him home and keep him until he was big enough to punch Heather in the face and do some real, lasting damage that would require reconstructive surgery that could be conveniently botched.

Zoe swallowed back all the nasties she had to say.

"Happy birthday, Beck," she managed. If only she'd said no on the first day of school. No to the invitation to sit down. No to the cigarette. If only she'd left the smoke hole before that wide gulf had been bridged between her and the Beckoners.

Zoe glumly handed Beck the card she and Cassy had made for her. She'd glued stars in the corners and framed it in baby blue fun fur. Beck held it in front of her face and peered at it. She fumbled to open it.

"It doesn't open," Zoe said.

Brady handed Zoe a drink. She assumed it was vodka, but she didn't particularly care. She downed it in one go. Yup. Vodka. One thing she knew from booze was that it made moments like these slightly more bearable, and that's what she wanted more than anything, for this moment to be even *slightly* more bearable.

"Is this supposed to be abstract art or something?" Beck was still trying to open the card. "'Cuz if it is, you kind of suck at it."

"My little sister—"

"Yeah, that's what they all say." Beck gave up trying to open it. She tossed it across the room like a hockey card.

"What's it supposed to be?" Jazz picked it up. She turned it upside down and then on its side. "If you look at it this way it looks like two giraffes fucking."

"Let me see!" Lindsay held up her hand. Jazz sent it into the air, but it fell short, into the whiskey on the floor. Lindsay picked it up by the corner and studied it. The paint bled down the paper.

"Now it looks like *four* giraffes fucking!" Lindsay howled. Everyone laughed harder, especially Beck, whose laugh grew shrill when she drank.

Zoe stood there with a mouthwash-ad grin on her face like she was able to handle being the butt of the joke. Her smile ached, but she couldn't make it go away, it was as if the alcohol had fixed it, like chemicals fix a photograph. She felt her cheek with the back of her hand; her face was on fire. She reached for another drink and downed it too, waiting for it all to be even just a little bit more bearable.

"I'm going to show this to Trevor." Brady grabbed the card as he headed out of the room. "He'll piss himself."

"I know where he is." Jazz pushed herself off the counter. "I'll come with you."

Fresh air, please, somebody take me outside! Nobody came to her rescue. They just laughed and laughed, like some twisted mental warp scene from a Hitchcock movie. Hadn't Zoe screamed those words out loud? Hadn't she? Apparently not.

Zoe backtracked through the sweaty dancers pretending they were at a rave and out the front door. She went around the back of the house, past a patio crammed with smokers, over a bridge spanning a little pond and along a sandy path lined with fairy lights. The property went way back, at least as long as a football field, but narrower. All along the outer edges of the lawn were little groups of people smoking whatever they were smoking and drinking whatever they were drinking.

Zoe walked further, past a small circle of wannabe flower children swaying to some retro-hippie guy's sad attempt at "Stairway to Heaven," past the last of the lights and into a dark grove of trees at the very back of the property. She sat on a tire swing and looked back at the party. The night was punctuated by the glow of cigarette ends, like lazy fireflies hovering here and there. Heather's house, more a mansion really, looked like a dollhouse from that distance, lavishly lit up, little dolls in their plastic party poses.

This was all wrong. Zoe looked at her watch; it was only quarter after ten. There was no way Janika would be ready to go home yet. Zoe counted the money in her pockets, but there wasn't enough to pay for a cab by herself. Through the trees, she heard a whimper, followed by a harsh whisper. She slipped the money back into her pocket and crept towards the voices.

The first thing she saw was Beck's birthday card, face down on the damp ground. Then she saw Brady, up against a tree, his pants loose at the waist, his wide back obscuring Heather, no doubt, whose leg he gripped against his waist. What a grimy slut.

Zoe stepped behind a tree and held her breath, not sure if she was going to laugh or gag. Then she heard Heather try to say something, but it was muffled. She peeked around the tree, just as Brady twisted slightly to the side. It wasn't Heather at all, but Jazz, her eyes squeezed shut, cheeks wet with tears. She shook her head, struggling to push his hand away from her mouth. He grabbed both her small wrists in his free hand and lifted them above her head. He took his other hand away from her mouth so he could grab hold of her leg again.

"Brady, stop," she whispered. "Stop, please!"

"Shut up!" He shoved her harder, knocking her head against the tree. "You started this. You can't just say no, not now."

Jazz kept her eyes shut and gulped back another sob.

Zoe opened her mouth to say something, to scream at him to get off her, but no sound came out.

She backed away, but then stopped. Was she supposed to stay? Where did she think she was going? Her head pounded. She lurched towards the house, waiting for her voice to come back.

She knew what she was supposed to do. She was supposed to stop the first person she saw and get help. She was supposed to yank the guitar out of hippie-boy's hands and smash Brady over the head with it. But she ran past without even slowing down. Where the hell did she think she was going?

To throw up on the patio steps, apparently. The alcohol seared her throat even more on the way up. She heaved long after she threw up everything in her, then she stood and wiped her mouth with the sleeve of her shirt, while everyone on the patio laughed at her, ice clinking in their drinks, bass thumping from inside.

Zoe ran. Along the side of the house, down the driveway, out the gate, a sharp right then flat out as if a slash horror villain was chasing her, she ran. She had never run so fast in all her life, but her legs understood what was at stake and her breath settled into a train-pace that matched her speed. She ran so fast that before she knew it she was at the bottom of the mountain, halfway home. She slowed at the crossroads. Which way was it? She bent over, hands on her knees, and gulped for breath. She tried to remember which way the taxi had turned. It was this road, wasn't it? Or was it the last one?

Who knows how long she was there like that. Long enough for the moon to shift higher in the sky. Long enough for Zoe to become very cold. The next time she looked up was when a car passed. It slowed, and then reversed towards her. It was Simon and Teo, in Blouise, Simon's ancient blue Toyota. Teo always drove because Simon had failed his driver's test twice now and had given up for a while.

Simon rolled down his window. "You want a ride?"

"No, I'm fine." Zoe was surprised to find that her voice worked now. "I just need to know which way is back to town."

"Town? Aren't you going to the party?"

"No, I'm not." She pointed down the road. "Which way do I go?"

"Uh-uh, no way." Simon shook his head. "I am not going to wake up tomorrow and find out that you were raped and left for dead at the side of the road. It would be all my fault."

The moment the word "raped" came out of his mouth, the image of Jazz shoved up against that tree came crashing back.

Zoe started to cry, shoulders heaving as each sob welled up and gripped her by the throat.

"Honey, you're crying." Simon got out. "Teo, she's crying. Get into Blouise, honey." He pulled her towards the car. "Tell me what happened."

"I was…I just…back there, I…"

Teo leaned across the seat with a box of tissues. Simon pulled out a handful and dabbed her cheeks. "Let us give you a ride, okay?"

"I haven't had a thing to drink yet." Teo held up two fingers. "Scout's honor."

"Okay," Zoe sobbed.

Simon steered her into the back seat. "Where's your jacket?" He scanned the ground at the side of the road as Teo put the car in gear. "Don't you have a bag or anything? Hold on, Teo." Simon climbed in and turned in his seat, taking both her hands in his. "Look at me, Zoe. Are you hurt? Did someone hurt you?"

"No," she sobbed. "I'm just lost. Just take me home."

As they pulled away, Zoe turned in her seat and watched another Zoe—Zoe the Beckoner, Zoe the weak, Zoe the bitch—standing at the side of the road, a terribly hurt look on her face, like why was she being left there, all alone in the middle of nowhere with no idea how to get home? Zoe hated her, that's why.

As they drove, Zoe leaned her head back and watched the streetlights flash by like stars strung in a tidy line. She felt heavy and desperate, panicky. This was what it felt like to fall, to hurtle towards the jumbled corpses of all the other losers at the bottom of the cliff. This must be what it felt like to be Dog. Zoe shook her head; no. Not Dog. April. April Donelly. This must be what it felt like to be April Donelly.

good morning

April was asleep on the couch when Zoe stumbled in, Shadow curled up in a ball behind her bent knees. The two of them were snoring. How could she sleep? Zoe wanted to shake her, scream at her, drag her up the mountain to that grove of trees and make her see what she saw. But she just sat there in the dark, wishing she was April, wishing she'd stayed home and watched some B-movie marathon on Channel Two.

Zoe went upstairs and crawled under the covers. She squeezed her eyes shut. Her heart pounded, racing towards morning with the speed of a silk train. She turned the light on and reached for her diary and spent two hours writing it all out. All of it, from that first stupid cigarette and Beck's eight ball matches right down to when she'd gotten home and watched April sleeping on the couch. She felt a little better. Her heartbeat had slowed, but still, she lay awake for hours. Every time her eyes drifted closed and she took a deep breath of sleep, she'd hear Jazz's thin whispers again. *No, Brady, stop, please.*

When she did finally fall asleep, it was after dawn. She fell fast into her favorite dream, of swimming in the ocean at night, on her back, staring up at the stars. But it morphed into a nightmare. The water vanished and she fell through a deep black nothingness towards the ocean floor, jolting awake just before she would've smashed head first into the jagged rocky bottom.

The house was silent, except for the patter of rain on the roof. There was a note on Cassy's pillow in her crib that said April had gone to babysit at number twenty-three and that Cassy was with Barb. Just above her signature she'd written, "Hope you had a great time at the party." Zoe ripped up the note into tiny pieces and flushed them down the toilet.

It was amazing, really. Her eyeballs had seen an awful thing, yet they kept on seeing everything else too, like walls and dressers, the clothes she was pulling on, the ground under her feet. Zoe had always thought that once she'd seen something awful, she'd keep seeing it, like those TVs with the little box in the corner with one image running while another one takes up the rest of the screen. But it wasn't like that; already her eyes had begun to forget, so fast that by the time she knocked on April's door, Zoe was losing details of the night before.

Had Jazz really been struggling? Maybe she'd seen a slice of something that had been going on for a while, maybe Jazz and Brady were doing all kinds of things on the sly and what she'd seen was just a lovers' spat? But if she'd seen a lovers' spat, why did she feel so dirty? Why did her skin crawl when the images replayed themselves? The tree. Her hands. His legs. And their voices, ringing in her ears like an infection. Ice clinking against glass. The moon creeping over the mountain. "Stairway to Heaven" on that out-of-tune guitar, a twisted soundtrack to a fucked-up night.

April's father opened the door, dressed in his neatly pressed paramedic uniform. He smelled of spicy cologne, and after he shook her hand and introduced himself, she smelled it on her fingers.

"My goodness, John, bring her inside." Barb pushed past him and pulled Zoe inside. "Look at you, you're soaked!" She handed Zoe a towel. Zoe hadn't even noticed it was raining.

She did notice the holographic Jesus portrait hanging in the dining room; look at it one way and he's handing out loaves and fish, move a little and he has his head bowed, hands clasped in prayer.

"You're up bright and early. April said you might want to sleep in." Barb ushered Zoe past a display of framed embroidered bible verses and into Lewis's room, where he was entertaining Cassy with an elaborate racetrack set up and a tub of Matchbox cars. "So you had a good time?"

"Not really."

Barb scooped Cassy off the floor and slipped her into her jacket and boots, carrying on as if Zoe had had announced that she'd had the time of her life.

"I don't know why April doesn't go to parties. I never missed one when I was her age. I loved high school. I was a cheerleader in my senior year, if you can believe that."

"A cheerleader?" Why would anyone recall that as a good thing?

"Well, I wasn't always like this." She fingered a gold cross below her double chin. "I used to be a size six. But when you have babies, your body changes and it doesn't change back."

"Do you remember any cheers?" Zoe forced herself to be polite. None of this was Barb's fault, after all.

"Of course I do." She set Cassy back on the floor in front of Lewis, then jumped into position, legs apart, thick fists gripping imaginary pom-poms, waving crazy-eights above her head. "C-E-N-T-R-aaaaaA-L!" Lewis dropped his cars and gawked at his mother. Barb bent at the waist and rose slowly, a look of grim victory on her face. "WE KILL! KILL! KILL! KILL!" She bent again, wheezing as she rose up for the last time, "CENTRAL GLADIATORS, GO! GO! GO!"

"You've still got it," Zoe managed to say. "Wow."

"Thank you." Barb panted. "It's a lot of fun. I tell April she should try out, but she just hides behind her hair and says, 'Not a chance, Mom.' But I think she'd be good at it. Don't you think? She's so slim."

"Hmm." Zoe tried to imagine Dog kicking up her scabby knees, belting out the chants with a sardonic grin. "I guess."

"Well, I think so." Barb reached down and tousled Lewis' red hair. "These are the best years of your life. I don't think you kids realize that. Say good-bye, Lewis."

"Good-bye Lewis." He stuck his tongue in the gap where his two front teeth had been and grinned.

All the way to Fraser House, Zoe argued with herself. Should she tell Alice? Should she keep quiet? She went back and forth: tell her, don't tell her, tell her, don't tell her.

If Zoe told Alice, what would Alice do anyway? It was so hard to tell with her, she could be so self-righteous about some things and so whatever-who-the-hell-cares about others. Would she call the cops? Would her face fall in defeat? Lips tighten? Would she say something like, "Aw, hon, did I raise you to stand by like that when someone's being hurt? Is that what I taught you?" Or would she tell Zoe that teenagers will be teenagers and what she saw was just real life happening as it does, whether you want it to or not?

Alice wouldn't understand.

Zoe let the last block decide; whatever foot took the last step would decide for her. Left foot: she'd tell Alice. Right foot: she wouldn't tell Alice. Left, right, left, right, up the steps, left, right, the intercom was an arm's length away, left, right…left. Could she fit one more step? Not honestly. Left foot it was. Tell her.

If she turned around and went back a couple blocks would she end up on her right foot instead?

Cassy stretched her arm towards the intercom buzzer. "My do it."

Zoe lifted her up. She knew Alice would see them on the little monitor intercom inside, so she tried to look normal. The intercom engaged, but all she could hear was Saturday morning cartoons blaring in the background, then a little kid's voice.

"Hi?"

Then a woman's voice, "Raleigh, get away from there!"

Then Alice's. "Off you go, Raleigh." Zoe could already tell her mother was in hyper-efficiency mode. "Hey you two, I'll come down and let you in. Hang on a sec."

Zoe pretended she was a Mrs. Potato Head with a red plastic lipstick grin stuck in her mouth hole.

It was a few minutes before Alice opened the door. Zoe's smile was slipping, but Alice didn't notice. She barely opened the door before whipping back up the stairs, two at a time. "Lock up behind you. I've got to get back to the pancakes."

She left Zoe alone on the landing, still trying to force a hello out of her Mrs. Potato Head grin.

Cassy tackled the stairs on all fours ahead of Zoe. Zoe forced herself to follow her up. All conversation stopped when they reached the top of the stairs. A handful of raggedy adults sat around one end of the long dining table, working on a jigsaw puzzle with pieces no bigger than nickels. Another half dozen residents were out on the deck, smoking cigarettes and sipping coffee, checking her out through the windows. Three kids were lying on their bellies in front of the TV, two brown-skinned boys and a little girl in a long flannel nightie, all of them wearing the same knitted slippers each kid got in their Welcome Bag, along with a stuffed bear and a toothbrush.

"Zoe?" Alice's voice carried from the kitchen. "That's Anita, Raleigh's her little girl. Carl, Ed, Josephine—those are her boys over there, Ricky and Dominic—Cleo, and you met Donelle last week, right?"

Donelle rubbed her hands together. "Bring that delicious baby over here so I can get a bite out of her." She held out her arms. Cassy toddled over so eagerly she almost toppled over a soccer ball in her path.

Zoe was completely stuck. Her mouth was open, but she made no sound. It was as if she was being quietly suffocated by the memory of the night before.

"Yoo-hoo." Donelle waved Cassy's hand. "You gonna join us or you gonna stand there and wait for a fancy invitation?"

Zoe ignored Donelle and focused on forcing herself to move. She managed to corner Alice in the kitchen. "I need to talk to you."

"Not when I'm at work, babe."

"It's really important."

"Then I'm sure it'll still be really important when I get off in an hour."

"Yeah, but—"

"Yeah, but nothing." Alice pulled a tray of pancakes out of the oven and added two more off the griddle. "This is my *job,* Zoe. I'm here for the residents. You've got me all to yourself most of the time. This is just not one of those times, okay?"

"But—"

"Not now." She glared at Zoe. A worker came in with a tray of dirty dishes and set it on the counter. Alice smiled her boss smile at him.

"If I don't tell you now," Zoe whispered, "I'm not sure if I'll be able to later."

"That is emotional blackmail, Zoe." Ah, another one of her tapes. A series she'd started listening to since they'd moved.

Emotional Blackmail—What Is It and Do You Do It? Emotional Blackmail at Work—The Invisible Tiger. Parenting and Emotional Blackmail—How To Parent Effectively Without Emotionally Blackmailing Your Children. It occurred to Zoe to ask, right then, if Alice really listened to those stupid tapes or if she just wrote down little sound bites that made her sound like she did.

"I will *not* hear this right now," Alice whispered harshly. "Is that understood?"

If she hadn't have been carrying the pancakes, she would've been wagging a finger at Zoe, something she was trying to do less lately, because one of her tapes said it was antagonizing and unhelpful.

Cleo held up her empty plate. "If those flapjacks were here on this thing I'd be able to eat them a whole lot easier."

"We'll discuss this later, Zoe. Keep an eye on the pancakes for me." Alice set the tray on the table and stood back with her hands on her hips and a great big as-fake-as-they-come smile on her face. "Chow time, people!"

Donelle glanced over at Zoe and said something Zoe couldn't quite hear, although she knew she heard her name. Alice threw her head back and laughed. Zoe half expected her mother to swat the air with an oven-mitted hand and gush, "Oh, aren't you just a peach!" Instead, Alice leaned over and said something back to the woman and everyone at the table laughed. Zoe stared out the front window at the cold rain, which was falling harder. She wished she were out in it, getting drenched to the bone, rather than suffer this.

The pancakes! Zoe turned to the stove just as the smoke alarm went off. The laughing stopped. Alice ran over and moved the griddle. Carl grabbed a tea towel and waved it under the alarm until it stopped. They all stared at Zoe, even the kids, the cartoon blaring behind them, ignored.

"What the hell are you doing over there?" Ed said. "All you got to do is flip the goddamn things."

"Let's watch our language around the children." Alice enunciated each word crisply. "Zoe Michelle Anderson, I do not know what has gotten into you. Go down to the office and wait for me there. And don't touch anything."

"You almost burnt down the goddamn house, Zoe Michelle Anderson." One of the boys pointed at her with a plastic boomerang held like a gun. "Pow! You're dead, stupid."

"Sorry about the pancakes," Zoe mumbled.

Alice pointed to the stairs. "Just *go*."

Zoe took a deep breath. She went to take Cassy with her, but Alice shook her head.

"She's fine up here with us."

"Yeah." Donelle cuddled her tight. "She's no trouble."

No trouble. Zoe imagined Alice cutting primly into her pancake as she left the room. "Zoe, on the other hand..." Wink, wink, nudge, nudge, and all of them laughing.

Which was ironic, Zoe knew. Alice was always going on to her friends about how good Zoe was, how she never got up to anything. She told perfect strangers that she was mother to the most well-adjusted teenager she'd ever met, like that made Alice some kind of parenting success. "Aren't I lucky?" she'd say, although what she meant was "Aren't I a great parent?" "I don't have to worry about a thing. Zoe's more like a little sister, really. I can't imagine her ever needing anything."

When Zoe heard Alice say things like that, it made it really hard to ask for help. When she was a latchkey kid in elementary school Alice told her to never, ever call her at work when she was home alone after school unless it was a matter of life or death. So Zoe didn't, not even when she wiped out on her roller skates on the cement floor in the basement and broke her arm. She'd waited until Alice got home; then on the way to the hospital Alice gave her the royal what-for for not calling her at work.

"But it wasn't a matter of life or death!"

"Come on, you're smarter than that," Alice said as they pulled into Emergency. "And don't go telling them you did this two hours ago, or I'll have to get Allan to babysit you after school. You want that?"

Ucky Allan Bates who adjusted his crotch way more than necessary? No, thank you. Zoe kept her mouth shut as the doctor set and plastered her arm. She didn't even cry.

"She did it just now," Alice told the doctor, more than once.

"Just now?" He shone his light in Zoe's eyes again.

Zoe looked away. "Just now," she mumbled.

"Hmm." He swung the light so the beam shone in Alice's face for a moment. "Just now, huh?"

By the time Alice came downstairs with Cassy toddling behind her, clutching a pancake in one hand and her dinosaur cup in the other, Zoe had decided not to tell her about Jazz. Not then anyway. Not yet. Probably and most likely not ever. In fact, she might not tell her mother another thing, ever, period. She was definitely and absolutely glad that she hadn't told her about the scar.

"Now, Zoe." Alice sat in the other swivel chair and leaned forward, elbows on her knees. "Let's take a few minutes so you can tell me what's going on for you, okay?"

"It's nothing."

"Didn't sound like nothing upstairs. You might feel better if you get it off your chest. I'm here for you."

Alice was using her work language on her. Zoe hated that. She started counting the little holes in the ceiling tiles, anything to avoid setting her eyes on her mother's holier-than-thou, I-feel-your-pain look. "I figured it out for myself."

"There, now, you see?" Alice sat back and crossed her arms. "You don't give yourself enough credit. You didn't need me after all."

On the way home from the shelter, Alice stopped at the grocery store, leaving Cassy and Zoe in the car while she dashed in.

She was gone a lot longer than a dash. When Cassy started to howl after a while, Zoe let her howl. She sat scrunched up in the front seat feeling deliriously sorry for herself. When Alice finally came back an hour later she was furious that Cassy was covered in snot and tears and was gasping for breath, she was crying so hard.

"Why didn't you comfort her?" Alice scooped her out of the car seat and cuddled her. "Hey, baby girl. It's okay."

"What took you so long?"

"I ran into Wish," Mom said. "You could've come and found me, you know. You're not helpless."

When they got home the red light on the answering machine was blinking. Alice pushed play, and Janika's gravelly voice filled the room. Zoe pushed past her and hit the erase button.

"Someone sure has their shirt in a knot." Alice frowned.

"*Someone* is feeling *ill.*" Zoe stomped up the stairs. "*Someone* would appreciate it if you told anyone who calls that *someone* is sick."

Zoe slept all afternoon, a miserable sheet-twisting sleep that didn't feel restful at all. When she woke, it had stopped raining. She felt guilty enough about letting Cassy cry in the car that she took her over to the playground as an apology. April was there with Lewis, and Shadow too, of course. They'd built up a bank with holes along one side of the wet sandbox. Lewis was very carefully parking a car in each little cave.

"Hey," Zoe said.

"Hey." April took a handful of cars from a plastic tub and lined them up for Lewis to park.

"What are you doing?"

"What does it look like?" She lined them up by color. Reds first, blues, then blacks.

"Well, I just—" Zoe looked away. "I just wanted to say thanks. For looking after Cassy last night."

April shrugged.

"You were so asleep when I got home, I figured why wake you." Zoe nodded for no particular reason. "I thought you might wake up. But you didn't." Zoe nodded again. "You're not talking to me?"

"It's supposed to be the other way around, last time I checked." April eyed Zoe, and then glanced down the path. "So what, the Beckoner's are around the corner, waiting for some kind of signal?" She gave Zoe the finger. "How about that? Is that what they're waiting for?"

"I'm all alone. I swear."

"Uh-huh." April started collecting the cars. "That sounds familiar."

"Hey! Stop it." Lewis grabbed a car out of her hand.

"Put the cars away, Lewis."

"No!"

"Put the cars in the tub! We're going."

"Why?"

"Because I said so."

Lewis dropped to his knees and doubled over, clutching the cars to his stomach.

"I'm not going and you can't make me!"

"It's okay, Lewis." Zoe took Cassy's hand. "You stay. We'll leave."

"Fine." April folded her arms.

Zoe tried to pick up Cassy, but she was not about to cooperate. She arched her back and screamed, hitting Zoe in the face with her sandy fists. April watched for a second, and then wordlessly lifted Cassy from Zoe's arms. Cassy rested her head on April's shoulder. She sniffled and glared at Zoe.

"Never mind," April said. "You don't have to leave. I wasn't sure if you were really alone, that's all. I thought it was a trap. I just thought that maybe after last night you and the Beckoners—"

"Don't worry." Zoe pulled her jacket under her bum and sat on the damp edge of the sandbox. "I'm done with the Beckoners."

"Done?"

"Sick of them. Finished. Done."

"Done, huh?" April set Cassy down beside Lewis, who had resumed his parking project. "How'd you manage that?"

"What do you mean?"

"You can't just walk away from the Beckoners."

"Well," Zoe shrugged. "That's what I did."

"You might think you did."

"I did. I'm finished with them."

April laughed. "But they're not finished with you."

"We'll see about that."

"Yeah, we will, won't we?" It was bizarre, the two of them using "we" like that, like they were in something together, other than Mrs. Henley's Private Club for the Bright and Bullied.

April moved the line of cars forward, beeping and putt-putting for Lewis. Zoe considered telling her about the party, but the couple of times she opened her mouth to start, whatever she had to say fell out onto the wet sand and flopped there like a dying fish.

Zoe watched them play; Cassy driving a red fire engine up and down the edge of the sandbox, Lewis parking his cars, April handing out the cars like she was God of Small Four-Wheeled Things. In the moment, Zoe wished she were Cassy and the only thing on her mind was keeping all her wheels on the ground. Shadow stood and stretched. He came over and rested his grizzled chin on Zoe's knee. He smelled sour and old and wet. Zoe stared into his cloudy brown eyes, feeling her weight leaving her in a trickle, until she was thin air, hovering above everything, watching from a safe, untouchable place.

magic words

There were three other high schools in Abbotsford. On the Monday morning after the party, Zoe tried to convince Alice to drive her to the one furthest away from Central and sign her up as a transfer.

"What the hell for?"

"I just don't like this one."

"You're not in trouble, are you?"

Zoe shook her head.

"Zoe, I don't have time for this crap." Alice fought with Cassy's zipper. "Central's practically out the front door. You are not transferring. No way."

"I could take the bus."

"You could, but you won't, because you're staying put and that's that." Alice steered Cassy towards the door. "And if I hear you're skipping, you'll be sorry."

So Zoe hid in the Art room until well after the first bell rang, and then she walked very slowly to English. Mrs. Henley wasn't there yet. Neither was Beck or Lindsay or Jazz or April. Zoe had just about decided, with indescribable relief, that Beck was skipping, but then in she straggled, wearing sunglasses and nursing a bottle of water. Lindsay and Jazz followed her.

"That is the last time I drink that much." Beck sunk into her seat. "I feel like shit."

"You always say that," Lindsay said. "The trick is to stick to one kind of drink. That's what I do, and I'm fine."

Lindsay did not look fine. She looked pasty and bloated. Jazz looked the worst by far, though. She seemed smaller to Zoe, like she'd shrunk three inches and lost ten pounds since Saturday night. Jazz folded herself into her seat, legs tucked under her, hands clasped in her lap. Zoe tried to catch her eye across the aisle, but Jazz just stared at her hands.

"Where did you disappear to anyway?" Beck looked over her sunglasses at Zoe. "Did you seduce some unsuspecting film student from the college?"

"I got sick," Zoe replied, eyes fixed on Jazz.

"Yeah, I heard you put on quite the puke show on the patio."

Zoe willed Jazz to look up and give her some kind of sign that what Zoe had seen wasn't what she thought she'd seen.

"I don't know what's wrong with her." Beck looked at Jazz too. "She went home early too, or so Janika and Lindsay say. I don't really remember much. Janika said she was looking for you everywhere. Why didn't you tell us when you left?"

"I didn't want to wreck the party."

“It would have been impossible to wreck that party. It was the best.” Beck stopped talking as April came into the room. She smiled at Zoe as she headed to her seat. Zoe smiled back.

“What are you looking at?” Beck stuck her leg out, blocking April’s way. “Got a problem, bitch?” April ducked her eyes to the floor and shook her head. “Say the magic words and I might let you pass.”

April shook her head. She backed up and started down the next aisle, but Beck swiveled in her seat and blocked her that way too.

“Let me go,” April whispered.

“Those are not the magic words. Neither is woof-woof, bow-wow or arf-arf. I know those are your favorites.”

April glanced up at Zoe.

“Don’t look at her. She doesn’t have the answer.” Beck nudged April’s white pants with her boot, leaving a nasty dirty streak down her calf. “Look at me, bitch.”

“Please,” April mumbled. “Please?”

“That’s not it either.”

“Pretty please?”

“Try again.”

April stared at the pile of books she gripped in her arms. Her notebook was on the top. “Just let me go?”

“Dog doesn’t know the magic words, class.” Beck raised her voice. “Can anyone help her remember them?”

“Yes, teacher,” Lindsay piped up in kindergarten falsetto. “I can.” She stood behind April.

“Repeat after me…” Beck stood too, sandwiching April between them. “Dog. Smells. Like. Shit.”

April shook her head.

“Say it.” Lindsay smacked the back of her head.

“Beck,” Zoe said. “Leave her alone.”

“Stay out of this, Zoe.”

Lindsay smacked April again, harder.

Zoe winced. “Don’t hit her, Lindsay.”

“I don’t take orders from you, Zoe.”

"Come on, Beck." She put her hand on Beck's arm. "Tell Lindsay not to hit her."

"All she has to do is say the magic words and I'll let her pass." Beck was nearly nose to nose with April, her glitter gloss lips just inches away from April's lips haloed with too much Chapstick. "Isn't that right, Dog? You know how this works. This is one of Dog's best tricks, isn't it?"

"Just say them," Zoe pleaded. "They're just words."

"Dog smells like shit," April mumbled.

"I didn't quite hear you." Beck cupped her hand to her ear. "Again. Loud enough for the whole class to hear."

They'd all heard her the first time. It was so quiet they could hear Mrs. Henley coming up the stairs, her high heels click-clicking. "You're running out of time, bitch."

"So are you." April lifted her chin. She looked Beck right in the eye. "Rebecca Alexandra Wilson smells like shit."

Beck balled her fist. She lifted it just as Mrs. Henley pushed open the door.

"Good Monday morning to you all."

Mrs. Henley assessed the silence that followed. She lowered her glasses to evaluate the scene in front of her. She glared pointedly at Lindsay and Beck.

"Sit."

Lindsay looked at Beck.

"Now," Mrs. Henley said. She shifted her eyes to April. "April?"

April swallowed. She shook her head and sat down, back ramrod straight.

When class ended, April raced out of the room before Beck had even put her pen down.

"Whatever." Beck winked at Lindsay. "She can't hide forever."

That was Zoe's plan, to hide forever. First step: steer clear of the smoke hole. At lunch she headed for the ravine, hoping Simon and Teo might be there. She took the long way around the back of the gym, down a trail she'd only been on once before. Halfway down, the rain splattering on the canopy of trees, she saw Jazz sitting on the bench at the bottom. She didn't have a jacket on, and her shirt was soaked right through to her bra. She'd undone her black braid. Her hair was plastered down her back like a long ink stain.

"Jazz?" Zoe sat on the bench beside her. "Are you okay?"

She looked up, her brow furrowed in anger. "I'm fine."

"You don't look fine."

"Well, I am."

"Where's your jacket?"

"In my locker."

"Why aren't you wearing it?"

"Because I don't want to. Is that a crime?"

"No." Zoe's heart pounded. She studied her zipper, trying to calm herself. She decided to take a leap. She had to say something. "So, did you have a good time at the party?"

"No."

"How come?"

"It just sucked."

"But why? Did something happen? Do you want to tell me anything? You can, you know. Tell me anything, I mean. You can trust me."

"Trust you." Jazz stared at her.

"Yeah. You can trust me."

Rain fell between the girls, filling the silence with its white noise.

Jazz pulled her hair over her shoulder and braided it again, slender fingers deftly twisting. She snapped an elastic on the end.

"Nothing happened, Zoe. Understand?"

"But you can tell me if—"

"If *nothing*." She pushed herself off the bench. "There's nothing to tell."

"Jazz, I—"

"Leave me alone, Zoe!"

Jazz ran up the steep hill, her tiny figure disappearing in the gray light at the top. Zoe stayed where she was, wishing the day were over with. Hell, she'd just as soon the week, the year, this life was over with.

When she went up later, Zoe could not resist the urge to see if Jazz had joined the others at the smoke hole. She had. Zoe watched her from behind a tree, ignoring the rain running down her jacket and soaking her thighs. Jazz was laughing with the Beckoners as if nothing bad had ever happened to her in her whole life. She'd changed into her gym gear and was wearing her jacket. She glanced over her shoulder, across the steaming hut, and caught sight of Zoe before she could duck out of sight behind the tree. Or maybe Zoe wanted her to see her. She held Zoe's gaze for a long, loaded second, and then looked past her like Zoe had suddenly vanished, or had never existed in the first place.

That afternoon, when Zoe told Simon that she wasn't a Beckoner anymore, he laughed so hard he got the hiccups. They were in Blouise, driving across town to the college library to research a science project.

"Zoe, you're talking about the Beckoners, not the freakin' Girl Scouts of America. It's not like you have any choice in the matter." Simon rolled his eyes at Teo. "Do you believe this girl?"

Teo nodded. "Some people resort to delusion as a way of avoiding shit."

"Well, this particular shit is not going to avoid *her*. It's like this, Zoe." Simon grabbed the Princess Leia and Darth Vader figurines from the line of *Star Wars* toys stuck to Blouise's dash. He twisted in the passenger seat. "And now, the dramatization." He wiggled Princess Leia. "This is you." Darth Vader bowed.

"This is the Beckoners." He set the two of them apart, facing each other.

"Okay, bye!" he said in pure Valley Girl, waving Princess Leia's stiff arm. "Thanks for initiating me into your vicious little girl-gang and everything, and like, I realize that hardly never ever in a million years it happens, but now I totally hate you, okay? So like, no hard feelings, right? Um, okay. Bye-eee." As Princess Leia teetered off, he lowered his voice. "NOT SO FAST. NOW YOU MUST DIE!" Darth Vader chased Princess Leia back and forth across the top of the seat until he caught her and pinned her to the vinyl with his boot. "No, no!" Princess Leia tried to wiggle free. Darth Vader sawed at her throat with his light saber. "Take that, you traitor!"

"You're exaggerating, Simon. I was hardly ever a Beckoner in the first place. The scar isn't even healed yet."

"Doesn't matter, Zoe. Once a Beckoner, always a Beckoner. You get that scar, you owe them something."

"I don't owe them anything. I changed my mind, that's all. Why should that piss them off? I just don't want to hang out with them. I don't like them, and anyway, Heather hates my guts. She'll be happy that I'm gone. That's what she wants. That's what she's wanted all along."

"You'll notice they're not named after Heather."

"But she's one of them. She's practically second in command."

"Heather couldn't command anything more complicated than wiping her own ass."

"What she thinks counts, though." Zoe failed to hear the conviction in her own voice. "I can tell she has some say with Beck."

"Whatever you say." Simon tugged one of Zoe's braids. "It's a shame about your hair."

"What about it?"

"Two words. Five syllables. Lisa Patterson."

"It's not like that." Zoe fingered her braids.

"Hey, Zoe?" Teo studied Zoe in the rear view mirror. "Simon and I are here for you if you need us, okay?"

"Speak for yourself." Simon turned to the front. "I'm on Beck's good side, remember?"

"Gee, thanks, Simon."

"Yeah, well, you make your own bed, now you lie in it, blah, blah, blah."

Teo looked at Simon.

"What?"

Teo said nothing. Simon looked out the window. After a couple blocks, he turned and looked at Zoe again.

"Sorry."

"It's okay," Zoe said, although she did not feel that way in the least. Her life felt the least okay ever.

"I wonder about Lisa Patterson every now and again." Simon said into another silence. "She disappeared before the ink wore off. She was really pretty, in a kind of gymnast sort of way. Really little and compact, but pretty. But it's hard to remember what she normally looked like. I always picture her with the ink all over her, and her shaved head, like some kind of freak from the future. That'd be a good way to mark prisoners, come to think of it. You know, in Russia, in the prisons, they've made up their own language of tattoos. A whole language made out of pictures on their bodies." Simon put his hand to Teo's Gemini tattoo at the back of his neck. "I wonder what—"

"I'd rather not wonder about Russian prisons at all," Teo said.

In the back seat, Zoe had tuned out everything except the name Lisa Patterson. Lisa Patterson, Lisa Patterson. Would her name join the legend? Lisa Patterson and Zoe Anderson. There was a certain, disturbing, lyrical ring to it.

"You won't tell anyone, will you Simon?"

"What?"

"That I was a Beckoner?"

"Most people know, Zoe."

"Central is huge. Not everybody knows." Zoe put her hands on his shoulders. "Promise not to tell? And don't tell Beck what I think of them either. Promise?"

Simon patted her hands. "I promise."

Zoe looked at him imploringly.

"Zoe." Simon gripped her hands in his. "I promise, okay?"

on the roof

Zoe told the Beckoners that she had to spend lunch hours in the library working on her science project as well as looking after Cassy after school every day. That amounted to a couple of days in the clear. It could only last so long, though. On Friday, in English class, Beck slapped a flyer for a rave on her desk.

"Surely Cinderella must get a day off, right?" Her voice was tight, challenging. "We'll pick you up around midnight tomorrow."

"I'm going to Chilliwack," Zoe blurted. "For the weekend. With Cassy. To visit our grandparents. We made plans ages ago."

"You don't get out much, do you?" Beck snatched the flyer back. "How about you call me when you can come out and play."

At dinner that evening, Alice announced she was an alcoholic again. Zoe hated it when her mother did that. Alice went through long self-righteous phases of not drinking at all, and then she'd get to a place where she was damned sure she could handle a beer or two, and then a beer or two became a two-four, with a major two- or three-day binge to follow shortly. The binges were guaranteed to end in tears, and one time in lock-up with a Driving Under the Influence charge. Then she'd get all fresh and clear and determined to stop again. Which meant she'd spend as many of her waking hours as possible at Alcoholics Anonymous meetings, leaving Zoe to babysit Cassy for free. However, Alice got way grumpy whenever she quit drinking, so at least she was grumpy somewhere other than home.

This time, oddly enough, Alice was bypassing the binge stage altogether. She plotted her AA route around town, mapping out how she'd keep herself at meetings until midnight in the same way she might've planned a night of barhopping before. Zoe changed into her pj's just before Alice left for her first meeting on Friday night and was still wearing them when she put Cassy to bed Saturday night. They were baby blue flannel bottoms, with white sheep with little black numbers on their bums, and an old *Mountain Film Festival* T-shirt stained with chicken soup and hot chocolate, the bottoms mucked with ketchup from Cassy getting her mac and cheese hands all over them at lunch. Alice was out for night two of meeting hopping, and there was nothing on the two channels they got except stockcar racing and newsmagazine shows. Cable was one of those items on the when-we've-got-a-little-extra-money list.

Zoe flopped on her bed and listened to the radio until a hockey game came on, then she fiddled with the dial, looking

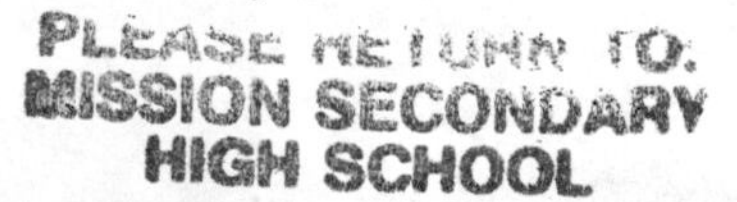

for something else to listen to, anything but hockey. She stopped when she heard the familiar haunting theme song of "Suspense," the mystery radio play from the forties, come through the static like an old favorite song she'd forgotten she loved. She used to listen to "Suspense" in Prince George, on Tuesday nights, when Alice was at Bingo and there wasn't anything on the one fuzzy channel they got up there.

The reception came in clear for a moment, but then it got choppy. It was a little better once she set the radio on the window ledge, but it was still crackly. She climbed out the window with the radio, careful not to knock the cracked glass with her knee. The reception was nearly perfect out there on the carport roof. Zoe kicked aside the garbage and sat under her window with the radio in her lap, antenna pointed west, towards Vancouver. Then she heard a voice.

"I thought I recognized you the other day." Leaf Morrison, editor of the school paper, object of Zoe's assured straightness, was sitting on the roof next door. "We're neighbors."

"You startled me." Zoe turned the radio down, only to find he was listening to it too.

"The best reception is out here," he said.

"Yours sounds better than mine."

"Then come over." Leaf pulled a plank of wood to the edge of the roof and bridged the gap.

"I'm looking after my little sister." The one time it was true and Zoe wished it wasn't.

"You can hear her from over here just as easy. Trust me, I know."

"Is that safe?" Zoe pointed at the plank.

"Tried, tested and true. I used to babysit Dean. He had your room. We'd come and go across it all the time. He thought it was great, like we were lost boys in *Peter Pan*. If a four year old can do it, so can you." Leaf held out his hand.

Without looking down at the one-story drop, Zoe set one foot on the plank, then the other in front of it. The board wasn't wide enough to stand with her feet together, not that she would've wanted to; she would've toppled over if she did. But she didn't. She made her way over like a tightrope artist, arms outstretched, eyes forward.

Leaf took her hand when she was within reach. That was the first time in the history of Zoe that she'd held a boy's hand, not including square dancing in gym class or recess lineup in kindergarten. He let go once she got her footing. Zoe lowered her hand slowly, looking at it as if it was suddenly new and improved and strangely unfamiliar.

"I think I'll go back the way everyone else does." She just about slipped the hand into her pocket, as if to preserve its new state, but in the process caught a glimpse of her ratty, geeky pj's and crossed her arms over her chest instead, like doing that would hide the stains. There was nothing she could do about the slippers, yellow and mint green polyester hand-knit jobbies from Fraser House. With pom-poms. Red and orange pom-poms. Lovely.

"If you're smart and your front door is locked, you can't go that way."

"Then I guess I'm smart." Zoe did not feel particularly smart at that moment. "It's locked."

"Nice slippers." Leaf plunked himself down on a foam cushion. He patted the space beside him.

"Thanks." Zoe sat down, tucking her feet under her so she wouldn't have to look at the slippers, which she'd really rather toss off the roof.

She and Leaf were sitting very close to each other. She could hear him inhale, a little nasal sigh each time. They sat, Zoe stiffly, Leaf oblivious to her stiffness, and listened to the rest of "Suspense," although Zoe wasn't paying the storyline any attention.

When it was over, Leaf turned the radio off, and slowly tuned in to the awkward silence. He looked at Zoe, waiting for her to say something. Zoe stared out at the night in front of them, the traffic going by, a couple walking their dog along the road. She waited for Leaf to say something. She went through all her mental scripts, looking for something to say that wouldn't be stupid, or clichéd, or desperate.

"Can you believe it's October and it's so warm?" Zoe wanted to groan. Clichéd *and* stupid, straight out of a bad TV sitcom.

"I can." Leaf nodded. "But then, I'm not from Prince George."

"How did you—?"

"Wish told me."

"She's your—?"

"Sister."

"Where are your—?"

"My parents? I keep cutting you off, sorry. My dad lives in a cabin up near Lilloet." He paused. "My mom's dead."

"Oh, I'm so sorry." Cliché number two.

"I don't remember her." Leaf looked towards the mountains. "I was Connor's age. She hit black ice, went over a cliff in her car."

"Why don't you live with your dad?"

"Me and Wish and Lionel—he's my dad, we moved down here after our old cabin burnt down. That was three years ago, but he's the only one who moved back. Wish got pregnant. She wanted to stay here. She figured we should go to school."

"You didn't before?"

"Nope. We were way up the valley. My dad doesn't believe in school."

"What does he think about you going to school now?"

"He's big into free will."

"Oh."

Zoe wanted to ask him a million questions. What did he do way up in the valley all those years? What was his father like? Wish? Leaf? Did they have middle names? He was so different, so interesting, so absolutely *not* a Beckoner, but then a girl's voice called up from below.

"Leaf? Hello?"

That would be The Girlfriend. Zoe did not want to look. She was probably tall and graceful, like Audrey Hepburn in *Breakfast at Tiffany's*, only less manic, more calm. She would be carefully made-up to look carefully not made-up at all. She would not be wearing slippers and jammies.

"Hey, April." Leaf looked over the edge.

Only April? Zoe actually sighed with relief.

"Uh...I brought the...papers?" She spoke so softly, her voice barely reached up to the roof. "You told me to bring over those... the columns I edited?"

"Sure," Leaf said. "Come on up. Wish'll let you in."

Leaf showed April exactly how to climb out the window, move by move, but even though she tried to copy him exactly, she caught her foot on the sill and toppled onto the gravel. Zoe couldn't help but laugh at her sprawled there on all fours. Not because it was funny, well, okay, it was funny in a thank-god-it-wasn't-me way, but also because she was nervous, and when she was nervous she tended to laugh at inappropriate moments.

"Sorry." Zoe helped her up.

"I brought the columns." April handed a folder to Leaf.

"I'll look at them later." Leaf dropped the folder inside. "Have a seat, relax. Welcome to my love pad."

April was sitting in the square of light coming from the room. Zoe saw her blush, and then frown, trying to cover up her embarrassment.

Leaf looked at Zoe and then April. "I was joking."

Zoe was glad she wasn't sitting in the square of light, otherwise Leaf would've seen her blush too.

"This is nice." April surveyed the gravel before gingerly setting herself down, legs straight out in front of her, hands folded in her lap. She chewed her lip. "Up here, I mean. Above everything." She laughed abruptly, a kind of half giggle, half gulp. "Balcony seats."

Leaf and Zoe glanced at each other behind her, eyebrows raised.

The conversation lurched along in short awkward bursts for a while, about the paper mostly, until Wish brought up a tray of hot chocolate.

"Not so fast," she said when Leaf reached to take the tray from her. "You only get this if I can come out and join you."

"Suit yourself," Leaf said.

"I always do." Wish arranged herself against the wall under a blanket with two pillows behind her back and two under her butt.

"Hey, April," she said. "Can you take Connor at your place next Friday? We've got a gig."

"Wish is in a band," Leaf whispered while Dog and Wish chatted easily about Connor and Lewis and recipes for oatmeal chocolate chip cookies and homemade Play-doh. "They're called The Fist Amendment. They suck, but they've only been together for a month. She's all, 'We've got a gig,' like it happens all the time, when really, Friday is their first gig ever."

"That guy who drives the tow-truck?" Zoe had noticed him and the truck around a lot. "Is he in the band?"

"T-Bone, yeah. He plays bass. He's in love with Wish."

"Oh." Again, Zoe blushed, and again, she was thankful for the shadows. "Is she in love with him back?"

"Getting there, I think."

For the next while, Zoe and Leaf talked. Later, Zoe would have no idea what about. She was so focused on getting the words out without stuttering. Why the hell was she stuttering? Shock and horror—since when did Zoe stutter?

April was getting up. She brushed off the bum of her pants.

Wish patted her knee. "See you next Friday?"

"Sure. Bye." April waved at Leaf and Zoe, took three tries at climbing back through the window, and left.

Wish waited until April had disappeared up the path to her house before she erupted all over Leaf.

"What the hell is your problem?"

"What?"

"The way you're treating April. I am totally ashamed of you."

"Treat her how? I didn't do anything."

"That's right, you totally ignored her!"

"She's impossible to talk to, Wish."

"I don't seem to have a problem talking to her."

"Yeah, but everybody else does."

"Since when do you have anything to do with 'everybody else'? I bet 'everybody else' doesn't even bother to try." Wish poked Leaf's chest. "She's not that bad. She's just unique. You're all for unique, right? Mr. Iconoclast? Or is it Mr. Hypocrite now? You didn't even say good-bye." She wagged her finger at Zoe. "And you, if this is your influence on my brother, then I don't want you in my house."

"No, it's just—I...I..." Zoe shut her mouth and wondered if she would be plagued with the stutters from here on in.

"We didn't—"

Wish held up her hand. Leaf shut his mouth too.

"I don't care what excuses you two think you have." Wish shook her head. "I really don't. What I care about is that everyone treats each other with a little respect. That girl is a brilliant writer, and she's great with kids, and she's sweet and caring and more of a human than either of you two are right now."

"That's not fair," Leaf said.

"Then act human."

"Wish, you know sometimes you're just...no. Forget it. Whatever. Sorry." The way Leaf said "sorry" was the same way Zoe said it to Alice when she didn't really mean it, as if he'd said "fine" instead.

"You're not sorry. You think I'm so out of touch that I can't possibly know the inner workings of your little world, all the rules and taboos and shit? I know it. All that girl needs is a couple of friends and a little help. She tells me the shit you people put her through."

"Us people?" Leaf shook his head. "Uh-uh. I never laid eyes on her, or said one word to her before last week. I didn't even know who she was."

Wish put a hand on his shoulder. "And if you had, would you've still picked her essay?"

"It's the Beckoners who do all that shit," Leaf said. "Not us."

Zoe instinctively covered her scar with her hand, although neither of them could see it under her sleeve.

"If you had known it was her..." Wish gripped his shoulders and looked him in the eye. "Would you have picked her?"

Leaf picked up a handful of gravel.

"Answer me."

He shrugged her off. "No, I wouldn't have. Okay?" He threw down the handful of gravel. "So, I'm not you. I'm not perfect."

"I don't expect you to be." Wish stood. "But I do expect you to be *you*, and not one of those brainless little sheep who can't think for themselves."

"I'm sorry," Leaf said. "Okay? I'm sorry." That time it sounded very real.

"Baaa," Wish said.

Leaf grinned. "Baaaaaaaa."

"If you're going to be a sheep, Leaf, be the bellwether. Be a leader at least."

Wish gathered up her blanket and pillows and dumped them inside. Then she said, as though she'd been rolling the thought around her head for a long while, "I wish she had more guts. I wish she'd stand up to them, you know?"

"She tried, in English the other day." Zoe was careful not to call her Dog. "But I bet you it's going to cause her more trouble than it was worth."

"She'll get over it." Wish gathered the mugs. "She'll survive."

"Who, Beck or April?" It was the first time since the Beckoners that Zoe had said Dog's real name out loud.

"Both," Wish said. "We all grow up and pretend we were never teenagers. Except people like you, Leaf."

"Hey, I'm as miserable as anybody."

"No you're not, babe. You're loved, and you do what you want, and no one hassles you. You're a teenage oasis." Wish pushed a chunk of hair out of his eyes. "Untouchable and perfect."

"Don't deny me my teenage angst, okay?" He grinned at her, a lopsided grin, eyes squinty, a little gap between his front teeth. Zoe had a bizarre urge to touch it; she had to clasp her hands tight together not to. "It's my constitutional right as an adolescent to be miserable."

"Whatever you say, babe." Wish cocked her head toward Zoe's house. "Cassy's awake."

"Ears like a superhero," Leaf said.

"Mama ears." Wish grinned. "Off you go, Zoe."

As she unfolded her legs to stand, Leaf reached for her other hand. Now he'd held both.

"Why don't you work on the paper too?"

"Me?"

"Yeah, then I wouldn't be alone with April. It would be much easier."

"Easier for you, maybe." Wish shook her head. "But it'd be worse for April. Three's a crowd, Leaf. Everybody knows that."

"Give me a break, Wish. I don't know what to talk to her about. It's easy talking to Zoe."

It was? Zoe the suddenly stuttering mess? Easy to talk to?

"If you ostracize her, I'll make your life hell," Wish said. "Promise me you'll be nice. But not condescending nice—real, genuine, human-style nice."

"Promise." Leaf crossed his heart.

Zoe didn't even try to sleep that night. She lay awake, hands behind her head, imagining the Dungeon, a bustling newsroom like in *Superman*, Leaf at the helm, pencil tucked behind his ear, winking suggestively across a bank of computers at her.

The next morning, Zoe was up early to beat the rush in the laundry room. She had just begun sorting the lights from darks when Beck strolled in on her way home from the rave. She was dressed in a long narrow black skirt and clunky silver boots, her eyes rimmed with heavy eye makeup, heroin junkie chic. She leaned against the doorjamb.

"Well, well, well. Having a good time with the grandparents?" If she'd had any Ecstasy earlier, it had long worn off. She was anything but ecstatic.

"We came home early." Zoe made a quick mental note of the exits. Beck was blocking that one, but there was a fire door beside the bathroom in the back.

"Yeah, and Heather's a virgin." Beck cocked her head to the side. "Why are you hiding from us? Why are you hiding from me?"

"We just came home early."

"Look, if you've got something to say to me, say it to my face, okay? I don't like being lied to. Or avoided."

"I'm not avoiding you—"

"Shut up, you are so. You never went to Chilliwack, did you?"

Zoe shook her head.

Beck stepped inside and shut the door. Zoe lifted Cassy out of the wagon full of laundry and took a step back. Beck slowly nodded.

"You're afraid of me."

"No." Zoe looked past Beck and out the window, praying someone would come to put their laundry in.

"Then why're you acting like I'm about to rip your throat out?" Beck nodded at the door. "Go, if you want. Nobody's stopping you."

"I'm not going anywhere." Zoe steeled herself, a hot flare of anger straightening her spine. This was just Beck. This wasn't the Beckoners. Just Beck, all by herself. Alone. Beck was just a girl, like her. She wasn't a monster. She had no superpowers. She was mortal like everybody else. Zoe hardened her expression.

"As you can see, I've got laundry to do." Zoe set Cassy down by the basket of toys in the corner and continued sorting the clothes, although what she really wanted to do was pour a jug of bleach down Beck's throat.

"What the hell is your problem?" Beck lifted herself onto the counter.

"I didn't want to go to the rave." Zoe loaded one of the machines. "That's all."

"You could've said that." Beck pulled a black bra out from the light pile. "What's wrong with you? You're acting all fucked."

"Nothing is wrong with me. I just felt like being alone."

"You could've said that too."

"Could I?" Zoe dumped the soap into the machine and let the lid slam.

"That's a stupid question, Zoe." Beck lit a cigarette. "You can say whatever you want."

Zoe wanted to say she wanted out of the Beckoners. She wanted to tell Beck that she was the one acting all fucked. She wanted most of all to ask why her? Why choose her? Of everyone in the world to pull into their mess, why her?

"I'm just used to being alone more. I like being alone."

"That's it?"

"Yeah, I guess."

"That's it." Beck stared at her, mouth in a tight line.

"Yeah, Beck. That's it." Zoe turned to start the machine, but Beck grabbed Zoe's arm and twisted it so the scar faced up. "This *means* something, Zoe." She squeezed hard. "Don't make me regret it any more than I already do." She threw down Zoe's arm. "You're on seriously thin ice."

Beck pushed herself off the counter and stalked out into the misty morning light, her silhouette fading long before her finger marks on Zoe's arm.

the dungeon

For days, Zoe dreamt of thin ice. She dreamt Mill Lake was frozen, and she was stranded in the middle, ice cracking around her, chunks tipping into the water, until she was left teetering on a small wedge; and then that too slipped under the water, and so did she, falling and falling and never reaching the bottom. She told Alice about the dreams, but Alice wasn't really listening.

"Maybe you're afraid of something," was all she said, eyes on the phone, waiting for another call she'd take in her bedroom, door closed.

"You could say that." Zoe tried to laugh.

"You can handle it. What is it? A test? Term project?"

"No, it's nothing like that. It's just that—"

The phone rang.

"Let it ring." Alice sprinted up the stairs. "I'll get it in my room."

Zoe pretended she didn't hear her. She picked up the phone.

"Hello?"

"Hi, babe." It was a man's voice. "How you doing?" He sounded like a smoker.

Alice cut in from the upstairs phone. "Put down the phone, Zoe."

"I just want to know who—"

"Hang up, *now*."

Zoe set down the phone and fought the urge to sneak up the stairs to try to listen at the bedroom door. It seemed that her mom's maternal instinct only ever kicked in when it suited her lately. Just the week before Zoe had tried listening with a glass against the door. All she could hear was mumble-mumble this, and mumble-mumble that, and the occasional full-on laugh Alice used whenever she was on the make. Zoe listened for only a moment before Alice flung open the door and snatched away the glass.

"You want me to start eavesdropping on your private calls? Right, I didn't think so. I catch you one more time and I'm taking away your phone privileges."

Not that that would've mattered. There was no one Zoe wanted to call, and no one who would call her besides one of the Beckoners, who she'd rather never hear from again as long as she lived.

That soon changed, though. Leaf stopped her in the hall a few days later during lunch, one of the rare times she set foot in the hallway during peak times, for fear of running into the Beckoners.

"I was beginning to wonder if you'd dropped out or something." His hand felt heavy and hot on her shoulder. "What do you have next?"

"A spare," she said, although she had Math.

"Perfect. Come with me." He led her to the Dungeon, a reclaimed janitor's closet at the end of the Industrial Arts wing. Inside was a sagging couch in front of a wall of shelves stacked with file boxes, two computer desks forming a square that took up most of the center of the tiny room, and a long layout table, above which was suspended the only light in the windowless room, a single shivering fluorescent tube.

"Those are the archives." Leaf pointed to the boxes as he led her to the layout table. "And this is all yours." He gave her a quick lesson on how to do the layout on the computer and then showed her how to do it by hand, arranging articles and columns and photos and headlines to fit within the structure of each page.

When April came in after the bell rang, Leaf made a great show of stopping and including her in the lesson. Zoe watched April lean over the table, inching closer to Leaf as he demonstrated how to justify margins.

"What do you do if you want to add something at the last minute?" April asked. It was about the fortieth question she'd asked in ten minutes. She hadn't shut up since she walked in. If Wish was worried about her not feeling included, she didn't need to. It was Zoe who was feeling left out.

"That's easier done on the computer." Leaf moved to the computer and showed the girls how to rearrange blocks of text, tightening things up to squish in a new block of space.

Zoe was acutely aware of the lack of air in the tiny room. It was stuffy and smelled of hot computers and old newspapers. Three people seemed too many for the space. She watched April babble on at Leaf. He looked like he was listening, giving intelligent, relevant answers, but he can't have been that interested. Every third question or so he looked across the computer at Zoe. She wasn't sure what his looks meant, or if they meant anything at all. He was definitely looking at Zoe, and Zoe alone, that much was for sure.

Unlike Zoe and April, Simon did not have a crush on Leaf, but as the weather got colder and the rain still ever constant, Simon took over the Dungeon as his personal living room whenever Teo was busy with football practice. Zoe had to get used to there being four bodies in that claustrophobic space, five if you counted Shadow, who April snuck in through the Industrial Arts bay door after school, even though Simon was allergic. He loved Shadow, though, so he never complained about the sneezing fits or how often he had to leave the room to wash his hands after touching him. He might have warmed up to Shadow after so many years of lumping him into the same pathetic space April occupied in the world, but he did not warm up to April, nor did she warm up to him.

"Don't put that there. Do it like this." He nudged April and Zoe aside and began rearranging the photo spread Zoe was putting together for the basketball tournament Central had won two days before. "Ta da!" He stood back and admired his work.

"Very artsy, Simon." Zoe winked at him.

April shook her head. "Too much white space."

"Less busy." Simon frowned at her. "The eye needs a rest."

"It looks vacuous." April turned away.

"Ooo, such a big word for such a little girl."

Zoe gripped Simon's wrist. "Leave it, Simon."

Simon cupped his hands around Zoe's ear and whispered, "That loser is pushing my buttons. I'm just about ready to hissy fit all over her."

"*She* has every right to be here."

"So do I. I'm your friend."

"Yeah, but she's the assistant editor."

"Yeah, so what? I'm your friend. If she had any friends, they could be in here too. But she doesn't have any friends, poor thing."

"Leave her alone, Simon. She has way more right to be here than you do."

Simon feigned being stabbed in the heart. He stumbled back to the couch, where he sat in silence, flipping through magazines, ignoring Zoe altogether.

After that, whenever Simon was there, April found a reason to leave, unless Leaf was there too. She never left if Leaf was there. In fact, if Leaf was there, she never left his side. It was almost funny, if it weren't so pathetic, the way she followed Leaf around the tiny room, Shadow following her, the three of them making up a little convoy passing between layout table, computer desk, couch and back. After a while, even Shadow realized the room was too small to follow April around. He gave up and claimed one end of the couch, resting his head on his paws and following April with his eyes instead.

Simon did hissy fit all over April, but not until the week before Halloween. Simon and Teo were forming a Gay/Straight Alliance, and wanted to run an ad in the paper about the first meeting. He and Leaf were scrolling through the layout on the computer, looking for a place to fit it in. April was unusually silent. Just as they'd decided to put it under the ad for the Halloween dance, she piped up.

"There's no room for it there."

"Sure there is." Simon didn't bother to look up at her. "We'll take out your editorial on the SPCA's new no-kill policy."

"No, you won't."

"I'm joking."

"You were not."

"Okay, I wasn't." Simon shrugged. "It's a boring editorial. It would've been more interesting to do a scathing exposé before they stopped murdering animals."

April looked down at last week's paper laying open in front of her. "Your ad shouldn't go in at all."

"Oh yeah?"

April nodded.

"How come?"

"It's sick."

"Excuse me?" Simon straightened. He put his hands on his hips. "Would you repeat that please?"

"It's sick."

"Sick?"

"That's right." April fingered the cross at her throat. "It's unnatural. I bet the school has a policy against it."

"Against what?"

"You know what."

"No." Simon shook his head. "Tell me."

"Against people like you."

Zoe winced. She and Leaf widened their eyes.

"Stand back," Leaf whispered.

"Oh. People like *me*. Oh." Simon crossed the room and leaned over April. "You know what, little miss fundamentalist? The *world* has a policy against people like you. At least us queers stick together. You losers have nobody but your lonesome lame-ass selves. How pathetic is that?"

"Simon—" Leaf started. Simon held up a silencing hand. He picked up April's cross as if it were a dead bug. Shadow growled from the couch, hackles raised, although he didn't bother lifting his head.

"This is supposed to mean tolerance and love, isn't it?" Simon dropped the cross. "Maybe you should be wearing it upside down, seeing as how you've got it all ass backwards."

"It says right in the bible—"

Again, Simon held up his hand for her to stop. "Please, before you make yourself out to look a hell of a lot less smart than Leaf claims you to be, shut the hell up."

April abruptly stood. Simon took a step back, arms up, making sure no part of her touched any part of him. April glanced at Leaf, then Zoe, and then back to Leaf. Neither of them said a word. April grabbed her notebook and left the room. Shadow reluctantly slid off the couch and stretched his legs before trotting out the door behind her.

Simon leaned out into the hall. "And don't come back until you've miraculously recovered from your tragic case of homophobia!"

"She works here," Leaf said as Simon grinned triumphantly at them. "You don't."

"You can't employ a homophobe," Simon said. "It's unconstitutional."

"What about freedom of religion?"

"What about hate mongering?"

"What about freedom of expression?"

"So the three guys who bashed my head into the pavement last spring?" What little color there was drained from Simon's cheeks. "They were expressing their freedom?"

"Come on, you two." Zoe placed herself between Leaf and Simon. "That's enough."

Zoe knew she should be feeling something for Simon. She knew how hard it was for him to talk about being bashed. It was like her empathy had been turned off though, because all she could think about was that Simon had said, and she had heard correctly, that Leaf had told him how smart April was. He talked to Simon about April? Then what about her? What about the glances? What about how he inched up right close to her when they were working on the computer together? Did he ever talk to Simon about her?

The next day April apologized to Simon and told him that she'd pray every day for him to stop being gay.

"I couldn't care less how much you pray for me," Simon said. "Frankly, I'd love to see your warped version of God try."

Zoe had to give April credit for resisting Simon's invitation to volley. Zoe thought April's praying was weird, but if it made April less of a Bible-thumper around Simon, then great.

The truce lasted less than one day.

Simon and April's fresh battle was over the subject of Halloween. April had put up with all the Halloween content in the paper, but she was putting her foot down and refusing to allow Simon to decorate the Dungeon with the fake cobwebs and cardboard tombstones he'd custom-made for each of them and Shadow.

"Halloween is satanic," April said. "No way."

"Oh, LORD," Simon said before putting his palm to his chest. "Oh no, my mistake. You think he's on YOUR side."

April would settle at nothing less than Simon ripping up her and Shadow's tombstones. Simon responded by tearing them up into the tiniest pieces he could manage.

"Some thanks." He dumped the shreds into the recycling bin. "That's the last time I do something nice for you, April." He patted Shadow on the head. "But not you, old grubby. We can't blame you for having a Jesus-freak mommy."

Once again, Zoe was impressed at April's ability to let an insult slide. Her capacity to ignore—was that a good thing? Or a bad thing?

April agreed to let Simon put the others outside in the hall, until Zoe reminded him that the Beckoners didn't know she was working on the paper and she'd like to keep it that way.

"I'll take mine home?" Zoe said, as a kind of apology.

"Fine." Simon threw the fake cobwebs into the trash. "I don't care."

Simon stewed in self-pity on the couch for a while, and then he said, "Leaf has a crush on you."

Both April and Zoe looked up at once.

"Zoe." The way Simon said her name made it perfectly clear that he was choosing this precise moment to deliver this information as a direct hit against April. It was no secret that she was glitched over Leaf: the way she followed him around, the strange moony smile she reserved just for him, her nervous fluttering whenever he was in the room.

April slumped forward a little, as if he'd stabbed her with the ballpoint pen he was balancing on his knuckles.

"Me?" Zoe felt tingly, like her blood wasn't getting all the places it was meant to.

"He told me he thinks you're cute."

April straightened. She turned back to her computer and starting typing furiously. Zoe could see that she was typing gibberish, that she was obviously upset, but she didn't really care.

"He told you I was cute?" Zoe flew across the room and jumped on the couch beside Simon. "When? What was the context? Was it something I said, like, 'Isn't that cute what she said?' Or was it me, like physically cute?"

"I don't know." Simon shrugged. "He just said you were cute."

"Cute, like ask-outable cute? Or cute, like, 'She'll never be pretty but she's cute?'"

"Cute, like don't ask me, cuz I don't know what kind of cute. God, how many cutes are there?" Simon raised his voice to match Zoe's high, excited tone. "Cute, like it's a compliment, so just shut up and take it, all right?"

"Okay." Zoe patted his knee. "I'll shut up now."

"Good girl."

Zoe rested her head on Simon's bony shoulder and was quiet for all of thirty seconds, during which April grew more fidgety, typing harder, jiggling her knees under the desk.

"Tell me more?" Zoe pleaded.

Simon whispered in Zoe's ear, "I think April's a little jealous."

"So what?" Zoe shrugged. "I could barely care less. Hey, Simon? When did he say I was cute? Recently?"

"A few days ago, I think. Monday?"

What had she been wearing? Zoe tried to recall every move of that day, but she couldn't think of anything specific.

"Hey, April," Zoe raised her voice, knowing full well she was rubbing salt in a wound. "Has Leaf ever say anything to you about me? Monday, maybe?"

April shook her head, eyes locked on her monitor.

"Aw, April's mad cuz Leaf likes Zoe." Simon pouted. "Poor thing. Maybe you should try girls, April."

April bit her lip. Her shoulders drooped. Zoe watched, waiting to see if this one would slide off. It didn't. April shoved her notebook into her pack.

"You don't have to leave, April." Simon uncurled his legs and got up. He stretched. "I'll be gracious this one time. See you later, Zoe." He kissed her on the cheek, and then blew a kiss to April across the room. "Bye, darling."

April took out her notebook and began typing again. Zoe watched her. Of course Leaf wouldn't be into April; she was awkward and arrogant and ugly. She smelled bad, like she didn't do her laundry often enough. She never said the right thing, and her timing was terrible. Like now, for example.

"Do you like him?" April asked all of a sudden.

"Who, Simon?" Zoe asked, even though she knew exactly who April was referring to.

"No. Leaf." April stopped typing. "Do you?"

Zoe didn't know what to say. Why should she tell April anything? She shrugged. "I don't know."

"You know."

"*You* seem to."

"You like him." April swallowed. "I know it. You like him."

"He's all right." Zoe shrugged again, trying to be casual.

"He's more than *all right.*'" April shook her head. She started typing again, to keep from looking at Zoe, sitting there all smug on the couch.

"Look, April, if you think he'd consider going out with you for even one second, you really are stupider than he *thinks you are*. A guy like him would never be into a girl like you."

"A girl like me."

"Yeah." Zoe wished she had a spare sock to shove in her own mouth. She heard the bitterness in her voice, the spite, but she kept talking. "A girl like you. A total loser. A bottom feeder."

"You're not exactly Miss Popularity right now, hiding from the Beckoners like a scared little mouse."

"I'm still glad I'm not you."

"Not yet, maybe."

"Not ever. I'm not like you, and do you know what, April?"

"No." April paused before continuing. "But I'm sure you're about to tell me." She sighed. "Go ahead. Tell me."

"It's your own fault that you're such a loser." Zoe was on a regrettable roll. "You bring it on yourself, like you were born with a target on your back and you go around handing out arrows for people to take their best shot. Like Simon, he would've been your friend if you weren't so weird and homophobic. There aren't many people in this school that would even stand being in the same room with you if they had a choice, but he's one of them, and you go all Christian Nazi on him."

The door opened, and Leaf appeared, balancing a tray of coffee and donuts along one arm.

"Excuse me." April grabbed her notebook, shoved it back into her pack, and headed for the door. She and Leaf did an awkward little dance, both stepping in the same direction twice, before April just shoved past him, nearly toppling the tray.

"What was that?" Leaf handed Zoe a donut, slightly soggy from the sloshed coffee.

Zoe looked at Leaf. "Do you like me, Leaf?"

"Do I like you?"

"Yeah, do you *like* me, like me?"

Leaf swallowed, his Adam's apple bulging. He set the tray on the layout table and stared hard at it, like he was memorizing it for that game where the tray would be covered and he'd have to recall exactly what was on it.

Zoe wanted to kill Simon. Leaf never told him anything. He'd made it all up just to hurt April, and now Leaf was about to prove it.

Leaf folded his arms and crossed his legs at the ankle, like he'd rather twist up and disappear than respond.

"Yeah, I *like* you, like you."

"Well, okay then." Zoe took a bite of donut. That settled that.

"Okay then what?" Leaf untwisted himself a little.

Zoe looked at her donut, wanting to throw up the bite she'd just swallowed. "Did I just ask you if you liked me? That was out loud?"

Leaf nodded.

"Oh."

"What do we do now?"

Zoe shrugged. "I don't know. I hadn't thought that far ahead."

day of the dead

The day after Halloween, Zoe woke up to the doorbell ringing. Alice called up from the bottom of the stairs.

"You awake, hon? It's April."

Zoe hadn't seen April since that afternoon in the Dungeon two days before. She groaned, pulling the covers up over her head. She heard Alice send April up. She probably wanted an apology. Zoe kept the blankets over her head, even when she knew April was standing in the doorway, waiting.

"What do you want, April? Look, if you want an apology, I'm sorry about what I said in the Dungeon." That came out nastier than she'd intended. She sounded like Heather. Zoe swallowed and tried again, softening her voice. "I'm sorry."

"I'm not looking for an apology." Something in April's tone was unsettling.

"Then what?" Zoe sat up.

"I want you to come see something."

"Right now?"

"Now."

"What it is?"

"Just come."

"Tell me what it is."

"No, just come."

"Fine." Zoe flung the covers off and put her feet on the floor. April didn't move. "Could you at least wait downstairs so I can get dressed?"

April wasn't dressed. She was still in her pajamas, the same purple nightgown she'd been wearing the morning after the Beckoners broke the windows.

April and Shadow waited for Zoe on the front step. April looked pale, dark half-circles under her eyes, which were red, like she'd been crying.

"What's this about?" Zoe pulled on a sweater Alice had borrowed from Harris and hadn't returned in the break-up. "Are you okay?"

"Follow me." April led Zoe up the path, her muddy slippers leaving wet tracks on the cement.

"Where are we going?"

April's silence was unnerving, almost creepy.

"What's going on?"

Zoe clomped along behind her in her gumboots, each step thunking in the early morning quiet. They stopped at the tall fence behind April's place. April pushed open the gate.

Zoe brought her hand to her mouth and gasped. A female mannequin with a noose around its neck swung listlessly from the branch of the apple tree below April's room. It was dressed in a stretched-out sweater and thin cotton pants, just like April on any given day. The blonde hair had been made limp and stringy, just like April's. It was even wearing the same yellow canvas shoes she wore every day, the kind sold for five dollars at the Budget & Bargain store across the street. A steak knife was stabbed into its chest where the heart would've been if it were real. A note drenched in fake blood was stuck to it. Zoe closed her eyes, unable to move.

"Did you know that today is the Day of the Dead?" April crossed the muddy garden and stood under the mannequin. "In Mexico, they build shrines to their dead people and celebrate all day, painting their faces like skeletons. Dancing in the street, partying."

"April, you have to call the cops. This is sick."

"Mexicans love their dead people. My dad says it's ungodly."

"What are you talking about?" Zoe followed her into the yard, trying—and failing—to keep her eyes off the grisly thing. "What has that got to do with this? Where are your parents?"

"My dad's sleeping off a night shift. Mom and Lewis are at the daycare. They didn't see it."

"Go get your dad!"

"No!"

"Then we'll go get your mom. Or my mom. We have to tell someone. April, this is a crime, I'm sure of it. Go wake up your dad."

"No." April ripped the note away and handed it to Zoe, the fake blood staining her fingertips. Written on it, in Heather's neat slanted writing was, "Do us all a favor, bitch."

"I would never, ever kill myself." April grabbed the paper back. "Do you know why? Because that's exactly what they want." She crumpled it up and ground it into the mud under her slipper.

"That was evidence, April."

"That was a *joke*. A prank. That's what the cops would say. Or maybe they'd say I brought it on myself, huh? That I must have a target on my back and go around handing out arrows for people to take their best shot." April gave the mannequin an angry shove. It swung stiffly, its hair like a veil, hiding its eyes.

"I didn't mean you deserve *this*," Zoe said. "No one deserves this."

"Then what did you mean?"

"I don't know, April." Zoe hugged herself. It was so cold, a damp cold much worse than the dry cold up north. Each word spoken was bathed in a wet translucent cloud. It was so cold, it seemed harder to speak. "What do you want me to say?"

"I don't want you to say anything." April reached up and grabbed the knife, wrenching it out of the plaster. Zoe winced. "I want you to help me get rid of it before anyone else sees it. And I don't want you to tell anyone. Especially not Leaf." She gripped the molded feet and pulled with all her weight. The neck snapped, dropping the body at their feet, the head swinging like a gruesome piñata. "Not anyone. Promise you won't tell anyone."

Zoe stared at the head: the wide-open eyes with long unlikely lashes, the mouth in a fashion runway pout.

"Promise!"

"I promise, April. Okay?" The promise was like lead. Zoe's shoulders slumped with the weight of it. This was not right. In the movies, this would've been the time when the kids who'd been struggling to figure things out on their own go for help. This was the climax. This was when the cops come and take it from there. This was the end. This was when the theme music swelled up and the credits started rolling. Only April wasn't going to let that happen, not yet.

The wind was oddly warm as they broke apart the mannequin and stuffed it into black garbage bags. Zoe had to jump on the knees to break the legs. She snapped the arms in half over a boulder, all the time wondering if this was what it felt like to break a real person. The crack of bone. The resistance. It felt wrong.

Zoe had suggested tipping her whole into the garbage, but April had refused. Zoe understood; if they'd left her whole, the horror would be bigger, an unintentional homage to all the murdered women found in dumpsters everywhere. If they left her whole, Zoe would think of her like that, lying on top of the trash, eyes wide open. This way it was somewhat finished.

The broken body bits fit into four bags, which they carried, two each, over to the bin behind the Budget & Bargain store. April tossed the bags in, one at a time. Zoe stood aside, hands clasped behind her back, feeling as though they should say something funereal.

"You're the Christian," she murmured. "Say something."

"She's not real." April heaved the last bag over the edge. "She has no soul."

April wiped her hands on her nightgown and walked away.

"Sorry," Zoe mumbled at the closed dumpster. "Rest in peace." She followed April across the road. The two girls went their separate ways in an eerie silence, without so much as a good-bye.

Zoe went to school early that day, to finish one of the extra assignments Mrs. Henley had given her and April that was due that class, and to take her mind off the mannequin. The last person she expected to see was Beck, but there she was, sitting cross-legged on Zoe's desk, a cup of coffee in each hand. Zoe had smelled the coffee from the hall and had known it was Beck. She could've turned around, but she didn't. She balked at the door, heart pounding. Beck glanced up at the wall clock.

"Aren't you early." She said it like an accusation.

Zoe didn't answer. She wondered if she bolted, would Beck come after her alone? It wasn't like Beck to work alone.

"I guess you would have to come in early, what with all that babysitting, and whatever else it is you do with your time. What do you do with your time?" She held one of the paper cups in Zoe's direction. "I got it the way you like it, honey and cream."

That coffee was like that cigarette on the second day of school. A peace offering. A test. Only now Zoe knew better. Beck knew Zoe knew about the mannequin. Take the coffee, and it would be an apology as well as a symbolic approval about the mannequin. Don't take the coffee and it would only be a matter of time before Zoe would look out her own bedroom window and see her own suicidal mannequin, with two black braids and a knife in her chest. What would her note say? "Traitor? Dog lover? Do us all a favor, bitch?"

Zoe's initial fear morphed into a tenuous anger.

"That's my seat, Beck," Zoe said, much to her own surprise. Zoe could tell Beck was taken aback too, by the way she pulled back her head, as if avoiding an insect flying at her.

"Gee, Beck, thanks for the coffee." Beck was still holding the coffee out to her. "That's really nice of you."

Zoe sighed. "That's my seat."

"So it is." Beck shimmied off the desk. "It's all yours."

Zoe took her seat and pulled the grammar text from her pack. She flipped to the index, trying to look studious.

"So, Zoe, what'd you do last night? Hang out with the man in black? What's his name? Autumn Wind? Maple Tree?"

Zoe turned to a random page and tried to read, but the words blurred. She waited for Beck to throw the coffee at her, dump it in her lap, over her head, down the back of her shirt. "I don't know who you're talking about."

"Yes you do, the guy in the Ramones shirt, who thinks he's better than everybody else?" Beck set down the coffee and yanked the book out of Zoe hands. She let it drop onto the floor with a bang. "Freak boy? Blue hair? Newspaper geek?"

"His name is Leaf."

"Leaf, how could I have forgotten?" Zoe could taste Beck's sarcasm like it was a vapor filling the room. "So, you still a virgin?"

Zoe leaned down to pick up the book, but Beck stepped on it. Zoe stared at Beck's boots, the scuff marks, the worn leather.

She considered grabbing Beck's ankle with both her hands and pulling her off her feet. She relished the idea, Beck sprawled on her back in a pool of coffee, hopefully unconscious from cracking her head on a desk on the way down. Maybe she'd stay that way. That'd be nice.

"Shut up, Beck." There was that flare of anger again, illuminating Zoe's black cavern of fear. "Just shut up. Just stop talking. Shut up. Shut up. *Shut. Up.*"

"Whoa." Beck took a sip of her own coffee. "Where'd that come from, huh? Feel better now?"

"I saw what you did." Zoe closed her eyes for a second to get rid of the image of the disembodied head swinging in the noose. "April showed me."

"Showed you what?"

"You know what."

"No. I don't. Tell me all about it."

Zoe sighed. "You're so innocent, aren't you?"

Beck toasted herself with the two coffees. "Always."

"Sure, you and Charles Manson."

Beck's self-satisfied smile melted into a slack-jawed glare. She set the cups on the desk and leaned forward, pushing up Zoe's sleeve, poking the scar.

"Don't think you can get away from this so easily, Zoe. I have an investment in you."

"You have nothing on me." Zoe wrenched her arm away. "Leave me alone."

"Never. You came in formally. You leave formally. I choose when. I choose where. I choose how bad."

"I'm not afraid of you, Beck."

"Yes, you are. And if you're not, you should be."

"Why did you do it?"

"What?"

Zoe had been about to ask about the mannequin, but instead she said, "Why did you initiate me?"

"It was a mistake."

"But why?"

Zoe sensed Beck's mood change, like the space between them had widened without either of them moving.

"That's none of your business."

"Who initiated you?"

Beck swallowed.

Zoe wanted to make a slice across Beck's perfect surface. She had the blade too. She knew who'd initiated Beck. She knew what had happened to her. She could only imagine what it would be like with a father like Mr. Wilson. As much as Zoe wanted to hurt her, she couldn't bring herself to do it so brutally. Besides, if Beck knew that Simon had told her, it would just put Simon in Beck's scope. He would be annihilated.

"Can I have my book back?" Zoe said instead of all the other things she could've.

"Get it yourself, bitch." Beck kicked the book, sending it skidding under the desks as the first bell rang. "That was your last chance, Zoe. You blew it." She picked up her own coffee and then Zoe's, and then she tipped them both into Zoe's lap.

Zoe didn't even flinch, she'd expected it so completely. She calmly got up and left to change into her gym shorts. Behind her, Beck laughed a little too forcefully, a little too loud and a little too long.

Zoe was surprised to see April there when she went back to class. If the mannequin had been an effigy of her, Zoe would've stayed home, pretending she was sick, anything to not face Beck. Zoe smiled at April as she took her seat, making sure Beck saw.

A couple of minutes into the lesson, while Mrs. Henley was busy writing something on the board, Beck twisted in her seat and sneered at April, hanging her head to the side, holding up an imaginary noose and sticking out her tongue like someone being strangled. Mrs. Henley turned around, mouth open, about to explain something, and then she saw Beck.

"I saw that, Rebecca." Her eyes narrowed.

"Saw what? I was stretching."

"I don't believe you."

April bolted from her desk and ran out of the room.

"April! Where are you going?" Mrs. Henley called after her.

April didn't stop. She tore down the hall to the stairs at the other end, her footsteps fading fast.

"Beck, gather your things and take yourself to Mr. Seaton's office. Immediately."

Beck turned red, from the scoop of her T-shirt up her neck like a thermometer, until her cheeks blazed. "Tell me what I did that's so bad."

"I do not answer to you, Rebecca. Gather your things."

"My name is *Beck*."

"Your name is *Rebecca*."

"Okay, *Jane*." Beck whipped her bag from under her seat and shoved her books into it. "You can keep this." She balled up her worksheet and chucked it. Mrs. Henley caught it with one hand.

Now it was Mrs. Henley's turn to go crimson. "I suggest you pick another time and place to have your little temper tantrum, Rebecca. It's very unbecoming."

"Well, I pick now." She stormed up the aisle. "Deal with it, *Jane*."

The door slammed behind her. The whole corridor could hear her rip down the hall, kicking lockers, knocking over the two metal garbage cans at the top of the stairs. They clattered and banged down to the landing. Mrs. Henley gracefully opened the door, stepped out and took a deep breath before hollering with drill-sergeant clarity and volume.

"And *if* you do not make it all the way into Mr. Seaton's office, I *will* find out and there *will* be hell to pay! Is that understood?"

There was no reply.

Zoe surveyed the room. Everyone carefully stared at their worksheet, including Jazz. Lindsay was the only exception. She slouched in her seat, gripping the sides of her desk.

"Do not even *think* about leaving this room, Lindsay McAllister." Mrs. Henley looked down her nose at her. "Furthermore, I do not want to hear a word from you. I am not in the mood." She readjusted her reading glasses and took a deep breath through her nose, nostrils flaring. "Now, if you would all be so kind as to turn to page seventy in the text, we will continue where we left off before we were so immaturely interrupted."

There was a compliant shuffle as pages turned, then cowed silence as Mrs. Henley continued with the lesson on dangling participles.

ashes

After trying mildly to convince her not to, Mrs. Henley helped April transfer out of that English class. Her new schedule put her in the same science class as Simon and Zoe. At first, Zoe thought she'd have to spend the hour keeping Simon and April from going at each other, but that wasn't the case. Something had changed between April and Simon, or maybe it was just April who'd changed. Maybe all her prayers to make Simon stop being gay were making her less freaky about it. But Simon had changed too. He was more tolerant of her, even gentle sometimes, and now that the two were more comfortable with each other, it became obvious that they had a wicked sense of humor in common.

The two of them bounced off each other like a comedy duo that was extra funny because they were so very different. They were so slick that sometimes Zoe just sat back and watched. April only ever hesitated in her comebacks when Brady, who sat way across the room by the window, caught her eye, or when Simon's humor degraded into the obscene or escalated into the outré queer, which April was still squeamish about.

One day, about two weeks after Halloween, Mr. Turner left the class with a quiz before leaving for another gin and tonic break. This meant nobody could leave right away. Brady made a call on his cell phone. Just as people were beginning to finish with the quiz, the door was kicked open and in came Beck, with Heather and Lindsay flanking her a step behind on either side. They shut the door behind them and surveyed the room, hands on hips.

Heather wiggled her fingers at Brady. He kissed the air like a soap star, winking at her, curling his lip in a way he must've thought was sexy.

"Ugh." Simon rolled his eyes. "Straight people are so gross." He waited for a reaction from April. She had gone white.

"You." Beck pointed at them.

Zoe wondered if she was there for April, or if this was the un-initiation at long last. Was it going to happen in front of the whole class? Zoe looked to see if Beck had brought scissors to chop of off Zoe's hair. She hadn't. Would she use the ones on Mr. Turner's desk? Or her knife? Did she have a way to get that past security?

"Get over here, bitch." Did she mean Zoe or April? April started to hyperventilate, a here-we-go-again slump to her shoulders, fingers gripping the edge of the table. She knew who they wanted.

"You don't have to do what she says," Simon whispered. He patted her elbow, like a little old lady might inadequately console a hysterical lost toddler. He pulled his hand away as Beck strode down the aisle without her bookends until she was standing right behind April.

Zoe released the breath she'd been holding and slumped with involuntary relief. They hadn't come for her. Not this time anyway.

"I'm talking to you, bitch."

April hunched over, covering her beloved notebook with both arms.

Beck stage-whispered, "Now let's not make this any messier than it needs to be." She stepped back and waited. After a moment, April stood, clutching her notebook to her chest.

"Simon." Beck nodded in his direction. "Nice to see you. I thought you'd died or something. Haven't seen you around much."

Simon took a second to square his shoulders. "I've been busy." His voice was strong and clear. He enunciated each word sharply. "With other things."

Beck smiled. "How *is* Teo, anyway?"

"He's absolutely perfect."

"That's nice. And Zoe," Beck smiled at her, "In case you're wondering, we haven't forgotten about you. We'll get to you. In the meantime, consider this part of your punishment. Dog?" She shoved April. "You can blame Zoe for this. If she wasn't such a traitor, we might've left you alone. Not now. Like I said," she winked at Zoe, "We'll deal with you later."

Simon sat up, tall in his chair. "I don't think you two have anything left to deal with from what I hear."

"Is that so?"

"Yes it is."

"How about you let me be the judge of that?" Beck grabbed April by the collar of her sweater.

"Get off me." April tried to shrug her off.

"Not a word," Beck hissed. "Got it?" She dragged April to the front of the room and shoved her against Mr. Turner's desk. "Good dog. Stay."

Beck clasped her hands behind her back and paced across the front of the room.

Simon finally stood up. "What are you doing, Beck?"

Beck wagged a finger at him. "No speaking out of turn, Simon."

"This isn't your—"

"You're only going to make it worse for her, Twinkie-boy. You want to help her out? You want to know what you can do for her? Shut up. That's what you can do."

"Beck, you're way out of line here."

"I don't see your hand up, Simon. You're speaking out of turn."

"Go ahead, then." Simon flicked his wrist at her. "Play House or Hitler, or whatever you have in mind." He gave her the Nazi salute. "Heil, Herr Beck!"

"Cute, Simon."

Simon sat down. His hands trembled. He leaned over and whispered, a crack in his voice, "This is barbaric."

Zoe nodded. "But if we do anything, she'll make it worse for April."

Beck hurled a piece of chalk at them. It burst on the table in a little cloud of dust that made Simon cough.

"Shut up!"

The rest of the class was already silent, everyone's eyes on Beck, or April, stranded there at the front of the room, holding her notebook like it was a life preserver, like it would keep her afloat somehow.

"Give it to me." Beck held out her hand like a mother demanding a baby spit out a marble.

April shook her head. "There's nothing in it about you anymore. I swear."

Beck kept her hand open and tilted her head in a way that said, "Don't piss me off" almost as clearly as if she'd said the words out loud.

"Beck, I swear to God there is nothing in here about you. Your name isn't even mentioned. None of the Beckoners are."

"Give it to me."

"Come on, Beck. After last year, do you think I'd be stupid enough to write in here about you?"

"Yes, you're that stupid."

"I swear, I haven't written anything in here about you or any of the Beckoners. Don't do this, Beck. Please. I'll do whatever you want. Just don't take my notebook."

"That's nice. Give it to me."

"I can't." She shook her head. "I won't."

"Do you really want to be difficult about this?"

April shook her head again. "I won't give it to you."

There was a pause while Beck stared at April, like she couldn't believe what she was hearing. Then she shrugged and said, "All right. Okay." She pulled April away from the desk and stood behind her like she was going to send her on her way back to her seat with a shove. "Have it your way, Dog."

April's eyes widened in surprise. "Oh, thank you! I'm so—"

Beck reached around and clamped her hand over April's mouth. April squirmed, trying to scream under Beck's grip. Her muffled cries sounded like the worst kind of movie screams, the ones that make you wonder what awful real thing the actor was recalling that made her stage scream so horribly real.

Simon gasped. "I can't watch!" He turned his face away. "Tell me when it's over."

Beck nodded to Lindsay.

Lindsay reached forward and ripped the notebook out of April's grasp. Once she'd lost it, April gave up her struggle and went limp, slipping out of Beck's grip and to the floor. She put her face in her hands and cried. Lindsay handed the notebook to Beck, who carried it like a sacrificial lamb over to the fume hood.

She placed it inside and then pulled out the same eight ball matchbook she'd used to light Zoe's cigarette that day so long ago.

April looked up when she heard the match strike, or maybe when the pinch of sulfur hit her nose.

"Please?" she whispered. "Please don't do this?"

Beck held the burning match up for a second for all to see, and then set the notebook ablaze. She pulled down the partition. The flames danced over the cover and then caught the curled up corners and really started to burn. The flames grew into tall plumes, twisting back and forth like slow belly dancers.

"Yeah!" Lindsay nodded her head. "Burn, baby, burn!"

Heather tossed Lindsay a cutting look. Lindsay coughed back another cheer and took her bodyguard stance, folding her arms and narrowing her eyes.

Simon turned and gasped again. "Jesus! Beck, what are you doing?"

"None of your business, Simon."

"It is so my business! You barge in here like you own the place, then demand our attention like you're some kind of royalty, just to pull this...baby prank? I've got—no, you know, we've *all* got—better things to do with our time that to watch you act like a moron. You're wasting our time, Beck. You are so lame up there, strutting around like some kind of walking wank. I swear, if you had a dick, you'd wank off in public all the time, you're so desperate for attention. You're pathetic. You know, there's counseling available for the shit you went through as a kid. You are such a cliché. There are talk shows about you on TV every day of the week. You don't have to do to other people what your dad did to you."

The class wasn't silent anymore. Some people laughed nervously. Others held their hands over their mouths, breath held in shock. Then there was Beck, whose control was sliding away from her like a snake shedding its skin.

"Okay, let's talk about perverts. Which one of us likes boys when they're supposed to like girls? Huh? You, Simon. Which one of us wanks off in the locker room when everyone else is in the showers? You, Simon. Which one of us has a stack of fag porn a foot high under his bed? You, Simon." There was a slight shudder in every word, as if she might crack and start crying at any moment.

The word "fag" took on a winged shape and flew around the room in a panic, like a trapped sparrow.

"You're a *faggot*?" Brady stood, his chair tipping over.

"Oh, surprise, surprise." Simon rolled his eyes. "Boy Wonder gets a clue."

"Man, if I'd known, I would've kicked your face in by now."

Simon took a deep breath and held his elbows to stop his hands from shaking. He forced a grin at Brady. "It's okay. You're not my type."

Brady hesitated, not sure if that was an insult or a compliment.

Simon turned his eyes to Beck before Brady could react. "And your point is, you poor, abused, waste of life?"

"My point is that no pansy-ass faggot is going tell me off."

"Stop it, Beck!" Zoe finally shouted, but it was like Simon and Beck were in their own little movie, oblivious of the audience. "Stop it!" Zoe shouted again, louder, but they ignored her. Zoe put her hand over Simon's, but he gently lifted it away, without even looking at her.

"Oh, Beck. My dear, demolished Beck. Didn't your mother ever tell you if you're always doing that…what do you call it… that really truly butt-ugly thing you do with your face that it'll freeze like that and you'll have to explain why you look like your panties are full of crabs? But then, your mother doesn't say much, does she?"

Beck put a hand to her chest and swallowed.

Lindsay whistled like a missile falling through the sky.

Heather planted her hands on her hips and spat back, "And didn't your mother ever tell you if you take it up the ass you'll get AIDS and your dick will fall off and you'll die?"

"So very educated." Simon sighed. "That's you, little miss fountain of information."

"Cocksucker." It was all Beck could manage to get out.

"Looking for tips?" Simon raised an eyebrow. "Ask Heather, she's the expert."

"Faggot."

"I love you too, sweetheart." Simon kissed the air, and then let his hands drop to his sides. He looked at Zoe. He had tapped into some reserve of power in himself, some un-tapped well of rage, but it was now entirely depleted. That's all he had. He was finished. Empty. He was passing some kind of invisible baton to Zoe. It was her turn.

"Beck, you're in way over your head," Zoe said. "When will you stop?"

Beck had been momentarily stunned by Simon's attack, but she had now rccovered.

"I haven't even started with you, Zoe." Beck walked slowly back to the fume hood. "You better hope you grow eyes in the back of your head, because when I come for you, it will be harsh. I promise."

"Leave us alone, Beck." Zoe struggled against the sliver of fear that had entered her voice.

"Never." Beck lifted the partition and stuck her hand into the pile of smoldering ash. She grabbed a fistful and walked back to April, who was still crying on the floor. Beck yanked her head up with one hand, and smeared the ashes all over April's wet face with the other. April sputtered and coughed. She reached up to wipe her face, but Beck smacked her hands away. April looked up at the class, her red face streaked with ash and tears and snot. Everyone was quiet.

"Never," Beck said again, her voice so low it was almost inaudible. She backed towards Heather and Lindsay, who were keeping an eye on the hallway. "I'm done." She glared at Zoe one last time. "For now. Let's go."

When the door shut, Simon rushed to April and helped her off the floor and into the nearest seat. The class stared at him, but he ignored them. The bell rang and the room started to clear, a couple of Brady clones spitting "faggot" and "homo" at him as they passed. Zoe filled a clean beaker with tap water and handed it to April. She gulped it down and finally stopped coughing.

Brady slapped the back of Simon's head on the way out. "You even look at me, and I will kill you, faggot."

"Like I said," Simon took the beaker over to the sink to refill it, "You're not my type."

Brady stopped mid-stride, inches from the door. Zoe braced herself, expecting him to go ape-shit on Simon, but Mr. Turner showed up then, nose and cheeks rosy. He pushed Brady aside and came into the room. He saw April, but he didn't ask. He went to his desk, ignoring them all, except to say, "If I find out who it was who used the fume hood without my permission, they will be suspended."

"You're dead," Brady whispered to the three. "You are so dead." He slammed the door.

"Get out." Mr. Turner said to Zoe. "And take your mess with you." He flapped a hand at Simon and April.

Once out the door, April pulled away from Simon and ran ahead of them and out of the school. Out the long bank of windows, Simon and Zoe watched her run for home, Shadow struggling up the drive to meet her, as if he'd expected her to come home early.

"I wish I had a dog," Simon said. It was such a strange thing to say. "I always wanted one." His voice dripped with grief. "But I'm so allergic." Then he cried, his eyes red and glassy. He cried silently, with no hysterics, as if he was just dicing an onion.

"Should I go after April?" Zoe handed him a wad of tissue from her pocket. "Or do you want me to stay with you?"

"I'll be fine," Simon rested his head against the window. "She won't."

girl on the roof

Zoe lay on the buzzer for nearly five minutes. Shadow barked furiously inside, but April did not open the door. Zoe went through the gate and hollered up at her window, but still, she didn't appear; there was only Shadow, paws on the sill, barking down at her. Finally, Zoe left a note for April to call her and went back to the school to find Simon.

He wasn't in Art, which is what they both had after Science. Zoe felt a prickle of worry; maybe Brady went and got Trevor and the two of them went after him. He wasn't in the ravine. He wasn't in the cafeteria. He wasn't at his locker, and he wasn't in any of the boys' washrooms. She found him in the Dungeon, on the couch beside Leaf, looking guilty, like he had been about to lean over and kiss Leaf, but it wasn't that at all.

"I told him," he said as Zoe shut the door. "I'm sorry, Zo."

"Told him what?" Zoe asked, but she knew.

"He told me what just happened." Leaf's face was stone. "He told me that you have the Beckoner's scar. He told me you're a Beckoner." He said the word like Beck said, "bitch," spitting it out like a sour candy.

"I am NOT a Beckoner."

"But you *were*."

Zoe glared at Simon. "You promised you wouldn't tell!"

"I had to tell someone, Zoe! You're in trouble. You heard Beck. Who else could I tell?"

"I can handle it," Zoe said, although she didn't believe that for one tiny moment.

"Oh, sure." Leaf crossed his arms. "Like you've handled it so far? Denial? You know what denial stands for? Don't Even Know I Am Lying."

Simon frowned. "There's no K in denial."

"Simon!" Leaf and Zoe said at the same time.

"Do you mean *notice*? Like Don't Even Notice I Am Lying?"

Zoe and Leaf glared at him.

"Right, I'll go." Simon stood up. "You two can figure this out."

"There's nothing to figure out," Leaf said. "Apparently Zoe can handle it."

"I can, thank you very much."

"Okay." Simon drew the word out and up at the end, like a question. "I guess I'll go now."

"I guess so," Leaf said.

"I guess so too." Zoe said. She wanted to leave with Simon. No, she wanted to leave ahead of Simon. She wanted to stalk out, flip her hair over her shoulder in that same self-righteous way Heather did, but Zoe's hair was braided and entirely unflippable. She wanted to flounce with a capital F. She wanted to simper. She wanted to be right, but she knew she was so totally and completely wrong, in so very much over her head, so far past the land of apologies that she'd tipped over into that ugly self-righteous place where it's impossible to say what she wanted to say, and the green blather that came out of her mouth was not at all what she intended. She wished, for a brief moment, that she was enough of a bitch to go home without finishing the layout. But if she didn't, the paper couldn't go to press on time, and there had never been a time in the two years Leaf had been editor that the paper was late.

"Okay, then. I am sorry, Zoe." Simon's hand rested on the doorknob. "Bye?"

"Uh-huh." Leaf and Zoe said together, and then glared at each other like each of them was the one that owned the words, and how dare the other use them.

The door closed, and Zoe was stuck with Leaf's stuffy disapproval fouling the air in the tiny, windowless room. Or maybe it was her.

Zoe was going mad. It had been almost an hour of itchy silence, except for the sound of fingers tapping keyboards. Her mouth kept opening for what one part of her wanted to be an apology, a plea, but then just as she was about to say it, the apology would get shoved out of the way by a snarky one liner. Unfortunately, it was one of those that made it out first.

"I didn't exactly plan on being in this mess, you know."

Leaf didn't look up from his computer. "Well, maybe you should've thought of that before you got involved with the Beckoners in the first place."

"You think I knew what I was getting into? I had no idea."

"No idea? Simon told you."

"Hardly anything!"

"He told you." He shrugged. "What more did you want? Someone to hold your hand?"

"Gee, thanks." Zoe's heart sank. Her tone of voice was so much bitchier than she intended. She wanted to say, "Yes, I did want someone to hold my hand." She wanted Leaf to hold her hand. Instead, she added icily, "Your kind words of support mean so much to me."

"Wait a minute." He was not going to look at her. "I'm supposed to feel sorry for you, just because things aren't going the way you want them to? If that's what you think, you've got another thing coming, Zoe."

"Another thing coming?" Zoe's jaw dropped. Her voice shook. "That's something my mother says when she's piss drunk and talking shit. That's something Beck would say."

Leaf shuffled through a stack of papers on his lap and shook his head. Conversation over. Zoe got the last word, but she wished she hadn't. She wanted to say more, but she couldn't trust what she'd come out with, so she resisted. Instead, she stared at Leaf so hard and imploringly he finally had to look up at her and say something.

"What about April?" he finally said. "How do you think she feels?"

"I know how she feels."

"Do you? Really? You think you know how she feels because now Beck's after you?"

Zoe was going to nod, but she knew where he was going with this, straight back to "another thing coming." She didn't respond.

"That's sweet." He nodded. "The Beckoners give you what, a couple of weeks of shit, and you think you know what it's like to be April in the world? She's been dealing with their bullshit for years." His voice was getting louder. "Years! You know nothing. You know less than nothing. None of us do. Being April would be like living in a war zone. Have you ever lived in a war zone?" He jutted his chin out. "Have you?"

"Anything I say will be wrong, won't it?"

"There's lots you could say that wouldn't be wrong."

"Like what?"

"Come on, Zoe, it's not that hard."

"Maybe it is. What do you know about it?"

"I know April is afraid. I know Simon is hurt, and afraid. I know you're afraid."

"I'm not."

"You *are*. Stop pretending."

"Beck wouldn't hurt Simon. They used to be friends."

"So did you." He crossed his arms.

"Hardly. He's been friends with her longer."

"Friends? Or was he just being careful? Staying on her good side? Afraid?"

"Simon's tough, and he's got Teo. He can handle it."

"Is that what you think?"

"Yes it is." Zoe crossed her arms too. "I'm the fresh meat. I'm in the most trouble right now. I'm the one they're going to un-initiate. What about that?"

"You expect me to feel sorry for you?"

"That's obviously not going to happen, is it, so why don't you just lay off?"

"Fine. I will." Leaf pulled his jacket off the back of the chair. He started for the door, and then stopped. He pulled a red slip of paper out of his pocket. He stared at it for a second, and then dropped it in her lap. It was a flyer for Wish's band, The Fist Amendment.

"They're playing at the Agriplex next Friday. Wish made me promise I'd ask you to go."

Zoe stared at the flaming anarchist symbol, wishing it were a magic eight ball with all the answers. "I guess you don't want to take me now." She handed the flyer back.

In that moment, the air shifted. It was less stuffy. She could suddenly breathe more easily, like an invisible window had opened somewhere in the room.

"I wouldn't mind taking the girl on the roof." Leaf cocked his head, appraising her. "I'd like to take her."

"I don't know her anymore." Zoe felt her throat well up, and a puffiness pushing under her eyes. "She moved, I think. To the Cayman Islands."

"Nah, she didn't." Leaf stepped away from the door. "I'm hoping she's still my next door neighbor."

Zoe had nothing to say. She just sat there, elbows on her knees, waiting for the tears to come. This felt like the few times she'd been sick to her stomach but couldn't actually throw up, times when she'd stuck her finger down her throat to make herself throw up, just to get it over with so that she could start to feel better. She couldn't force tears, though.

"Hey, Zoe? Can I ask you something?"

"Sure," she said miserably, staring at her knees.

"What changed your mind about the Beckoners? What happened?"

"The more I got to know them, the more I didn't want to." She closed her eyes and saw, like a movie played in speed rewind, that awful scene in the dark of the trees at the back of Heather's property. Her stomach flipped. "But you can't just walk away. Not from girls like them."

"What do you do then?"

"Wait."

"For the un-initiation?" He lifted her arm and pushed her sleeve up to look at the scar. Still raised. Still red. Still tender. "Then it'll be over?" He covered the four lines with his fingers. A rush of pure attraction pushed Zoe's queasiness and shame aside, making room for a sudden storm of butterflies.

"I hope so."

"This scar isn't the end of the world, you know."

"It feels like it is."

"It might feel like it, but it's not." He lifted his fingers away. "Do you believe me?"

"Not right now." Zoe wished she could say yes. "Not yet."

That scar would always be there—a reminder of this mess. When she's twenty, studying film, on set in the summer in a slinky tank top showing off the tits she finally managed to grow, calling the shots—the scar will be there. When she's forty, at the Oscars in a strapless evening gown, saluting the adoring crowd with the heavy award, lurching through her thank-yous—the scar will be there. When she dies, her body being prepared for her funeral, the man gently lifting her arm to wash her papery skin—the scar will be there still, and he would wonder about it and never know.

Zoe would never be rid of it. She started to cry. Leaf lifted her arm and kissed the scar once, and then again. Then he cupped his hand behind her neck and pulled her to him. He kissed her on the lips, and then again, parting her lips with his. He tasted of coffee. His lips chapped, dry. Zoe blinked a few times, and then closed her eyes and relaxed, kissing him back.

When Leaf left her at her door later, he kissed her again. Zoe hoped the whole world was watching. She hoped everyone had reason to be looking out their windows right at that moment. She wanted the whole world to know that Leaf picked her. Of all the girls he could've had, he chose her. Zoe glanced at the kitchen window, hoping Alice was at the sink, watching, but the window was dark.

Zoe floated inside, and immediately came crashing down to earth. Alice was curled up on the couch, clutching a box of tissue, sobbing, empty beer cans scattered on the carpet and coffee table. Cassy was squatting in the middle of the floor pulling stuffing out of a pillow and carefully distributing it around the room. Fluffs of it decorated the plants, the carpet, and the top of the TV, which was muted on a talk show, two junkie twins with buzzcuts lunging at each other. Zoe turned it off, picked up Cassy and waited for Alice to say something.

"Don't ask me, okay?" Alice blinked up at her. She peeled herself off the couch, and headed for the stairs, clutching the box of tissue. "Just don't."

"Ask me!" Zoe screamed at her. "Ask me for once!"

Alice paused at the landing, hand steadying herself against the wall. All weepy and puffed-up, she shook her head. "Not right now, hon, okay?"

un-initiation

By the next Friday, Zoe and Leaf and Simon had convinced April to come back to school. Until then, she'd left home in the morning and waited in the playground for her parents to leave for work, and then went back home. She only agreed to come back to school because Teo offered to be her personal bodyguard, now that football was over with and he had the time. Everywhere she went, he went.

Zoe never went anywhere alone either. At least one of the boys went with her everywhere too, usually Leaf.

The night of Wish's show, April came over to watch the kids at Zoe's house, because the band was going back to Wish's after and they'd wake the babies, no doubt. April had been invited to go, but her parents wouldn't let her. They thought Wish's band was satanic. April insisted that she didn't think the same, but she wasn't very convincing. That night Simon and Teo were in Vancouver for a Queerlings glow-in-the-dark bowling fundraiser that Simon was dragging Teo to, very much against his will. So, it was just Leaf and Zoe going. That was fine by Zoe; that meant it was kind of a date. They rode with Wish and T-Bone in the tow-truck to the Agriplex, which was out by the highway.

The Agriplex was built like a giant red barn, only it was meant for concerts and exhibitions and didn't smell of cow shit, thankfully. Leaf and T-Bone starting lugging in the equipment, while Zoe stayed with Wish, who had thrown up twice behind the tow-truck.

"Nerves," Wish mumbled, wiping her mouth with a tissue. Leaf came back and helped Wish to sit on the bumper of the tow-truck. She held her hand away from her mouth just long enough to gulp and say, "I get the worst stage fright."

"I've heard if you stick your head between your knees it helps," Zoe said.

Wish shook her head and swallowed. "That would just make me throw up again."

Zoe and Leaf enticed Wish into the building with promises of bottled water and ice. She sat with them backstage while T-Bone and the rest of the band finished the sound check. Leaf rubbed her shoulders as he watched the people coming in. All of a sudden he stopped. "Uh-oh. Look."

"What?" Wish lifted her head.

He pointed. "Trouble."

Beck and Brady and the rest of the Beckoners were at the admission table, fishing in their pockets for money. Brady was doing his weird slouch-walk, the one that looked okay in LA gangsta movies but looked plain idiotic in Abbotsford, especially with his pants jailing so low it was a miracle they weren't around his ankles.

"Did they know you were going to be here?" Leaf turned to Zoe.

"I didn't tell anyone."

"Who are they?" Wish had taken off her glasses for the show. She squinted at the Beckoners.

"Spawn of Satan," Leaf said.

"Evil incarnate," Zoe said.

"Whatever." Wish looked away. "So long as they pay to get in, I don't care who they are."

"Don't worry," Leaf assured Zoe after Wish finally made it onto the stage. "We could always sic T-Bone on them."

"What would he do?" Zoe said. "Assault them with some of his ancient Buddhist wisdom? Thanks anyway. I'll just lay low."

The second Wish started to sing—if screeching qualified as singing—her stage fright evaporated and she careened around the stage like she was on speed. They weren't very musical though, or maybe they were, but the treble disappeared into the rafters, so all Zoe could hear was a loud echo of what she imagined it was supposed to sound like. On the other hand, the crowd loved them. A mosh pit at the foot of the stage was a steaming mess of arms and legs so tangled you couldn't tell who belonged to what limb. Pop and smuggled-in booze sloshed out of bottles and cans; people bashed into each other like it was a newly discovered mating ritual. When Brady hurled his third beer bottle onto the stage, just missing T-Bone's face by a whisper, Wish stopped singing, a wail of feedback piercing the air.

"That's it, I've had it!" She hollered into the microphone. "Go pull your dicks somewhere else, right? I don't need this shit." She threw up her hands and stomped off the stage.

"Uh, we'll have an intermission now," T-Bone mumbled into his mike. The rest of the band stared at the crowd for a second, and then set down their gear and followed Wish into the wings.

The crowd emptied out the front doors, spilling into the cold evening and congregating in little cliques in the parking lot. The Beckoners were the first out the door, once Brady stopped swearing at Wish, so Leaf and Zoe jumped off the front of the stage and picked up all the garbage while the coast was clear. When they'd filled two big bags with plastic cups and other debris, including two pairs of underwear and a retainer, they hauled them out the back door to the garbage bins. Just as they turned to go back in, Beck and Lindsay came around the side of the building.

"Too bad you never grew those eyes in the back of your head." Beck stepped in front of Zoe, blocking the door.

"Get out of our way." Leaf stepped closer to Zoe.

Beck held out her hand. "You must be Leaf."

Leaf folded his arms tight across his chest. Beck kept her hand suspended between them for a long second and then dropped it slowly. "Well, it's nice to meet you, Leaf. Zoe talks a lot about you."

"I don't, Leaf. She's lying."

Leaf glanced at Zoe. "Zoe talks a lot about you too."

"Really? I don't know if that's a good thing or a bad thing."

"It's a bad thing," Leaf said. "Get out of our way."

Beck stepped aside, nodding for Lindsay to do the same.

"If you don't mind, Leaf, we need to have a little chat with Zoe. It'll just take a minute."

"I'm not her keeper." Leaf glanced at Zoe again, his eyes dark. "But I don't think she's interested in having a little chat with you."

"Zoe?"

Zoe shook her head, inching closer to Leaf and the door. "Some other time?"

"Some other time?" Beck laughed. "I'm not asking you over for tea and cookies here. This isn't a whenever's-good-for-you situation. I have things to say to you. Now, and only now, works for me. Understand?"

"Now doesn't work for us." Leaf pulled open the heavy door and waited for Zoe to go in ahead of him. Zoe didn't move.

"I think I want to get this over with, Leaf."

"That's my girl." Beck patted Zoe's shoulder and smiled at Leaf. "Don't you worry about your little girlfriend. We're not going to do anything to her that she isn't expecting. We just need to sort out some business."

"Zoe, I'm not okay with this."

"Neither am I!" Zoe whispered.

"So come back inside." He reached for her hand, but she pulled away.

"I just want it to be over with."

"Are you sure?"

Zoe nodded. "The waiting is worse. I don't want to wait anymore."

"We'll be twenty minutes, tops," Beck said. "Then the Beckoners will leave you alone for good. You were a bad investment, that's all. End of story."

Leaf looked at Zoe, his brow furrowed. "Twenty minutes?"

"Not a minute more, lover boy." Beck flashed him a smile. "Promise."

Leaf looked from Zoe to Beck, to Lindsay, and then shook his head.

"No. No way. I go too, or it's not happening."

"That's very sweet of you." Beck smiled again. "Very chivalrous. But that's not an option. This is between Zoe and the Beckoners. It has nothing to do with you."

"Then forget it." Leaf grabbed Zoe's hand.

"I just want it over, Leaf." She pulled away. "If it's not now, it'll be some other time when you're not around. At least now you know what's happening. She says twenty minutes. If I'm not back, you can come for me."

"Twenty minutes." Leaf took her hand and squeezed it. "That's it." He checked his watch, kissed her, and then went back inside, the door slowly closing behind him.

Beck and Lindsay walked on either side of Zoe, like wardens escorting a prisoner. They led her around the building to the back of the parking lot, where the rest of the Beckoners were waiting, perched on the back of Brady's truck, passing around a mickey of whiskey.

Janika held it out to her. "You might want some of this."

"No, thanks." The smell took her back to Beck's birthday party, the smashed bottle on the floor, Malcolm singing in his high thin voice.

Heather shook the bottle in Zoe's face. "Last chance," she sang, some of the whiskey sloshing onto Zoe's shirt.

Zoe swallowed hard, the smell making her gag. "Can we get this over with?"

"Sure we can." Beck pulled something out of her backpack. "This won't take long at all." Beck was not holding scissors. She was opening her jackknife. Zoe's hand flew up to her braids.

"Whoa, wait a minute. You're going to use *that*?"

"What else would I use?"

"Scissors?"

The Beckoners laughed. Lindsay slapped Zoe's hand away from her hair.

"She thinks we're going to cut off her hair, like Lisa."

"You're not?" Zoe put her hands up, as if she was being held at gunpoint. "Then what the hell are you planning to do with the knife?"

"Edit," Beck said.

"*What*?"

"Your scar, the one we let you have, the one we trusted you with, *our* mark? You're not entitled to it anymore. Really, you never were."

"It won't be any worse than the initiation." Janika jumped down from the truck. "You go along with this, and we're done. We won't have anything to do with you anymore. That's what you want, isn't it?"

"You'll leave April alone too?"

"Go along with this now," Janika said, "without a fight, and we'll leave you alone for good."

"Yeah," Lindsay cut in, "but if you don't, we'll hunt you, bitch. You haven't seen anything yet."

Zoe just wanted it over with. "Okay." She squeezed her eyes shut and held out her arm. "Do it." She waited, heart pounding, anticipating the sudden slice of skin, the shock of pain. Nothing happened. Zoe kept her eyes shut.

"Do it, Beck." That was Jazz.

Then Lindsay. "Go ahead, Beck. Do it!"

Zoe did not want to open her eyes. She could not watch, but what was happening? She heard Heather come forward; she could tell by the sound of her high heel boots on the cement.

"What are you waiting for, Beck? Give me the knife." Heather grabbed it from her. "I'll fucking do it. Hold her arm, Lindsay." Lindsay gripped Zoe so hard she could feel the blood slow down at her wrist.

She opened her eyes. She hadn't meant to. It was instinct. She saw Heather gripping the knife, knuckles white. Beck was backing away, eyes on Zoe. Zoe glanced down at her pale white arm just as Heather pressed the knife to it and sliced a deep line diagonally across the scar, and then quickly again the other way, a bloody X.

"Shit," Janika breathed out the word. "We weren't going to do it that deep!" She shoved Heather and Lindsay out of the way. Heather dropped the knife and stared at Zoe, transfixed.

"That's what you get." Her voice wavered. "Now we're even."

Zoe felt woozy, like she might tip over if even the slightest breeze came up. She pressed her hand to the cuts, blood streaming through her fingers, dripping onto the knife splayed at her feet, onto the cement in fat dark splotches.

"Let's go!" Brady leapt out of the back of the truck and into the cab. "Come on!"

"Here." Janika pulled off her bandana, untied it and folded it lengthwise. She cinched it over the X. "Hold it tight."

Heather had stopped staring at Zoe and was now staring at the blood seeping through the cloth and running down Zoe's arm, dripping off her fingertips.

"Come on!" Lindsay picked up the knife, wiped it on her jeans and pulled Heather away.

"You'll be okay," Janika said. "You'll be fine." She climbed into the truck and they sped off, tires screeching.

Zoe stood still for a moment, deliriousness slipping over her like a shroud. Her knees buckled and she landed hard on the ground, her hip hitting a concrete divider on the way down. The pain of that was nothing compared to her arm.

She lay there, hand clamped on her arm, conscious of every breath she let out, but not aware of much else. She didn't move until she could hear Leaf calling her name across the parking lot, the thin thump of T-Bone's bass echoing behind him.

"Here," Zoe mumbled. "I'm over here."

He couldn't hear her at first, but eventually his search brought him closer. He called her name again, panic rising in his voice. Zoe pulled herself up onto the divider. She had intended to stand, but she was so tingly she worried that if she got up onto her feet she'd just keel over again.

"I'm here!" She called as loud as she could. He saw her and sprinted over, taking it all in: the blood, the bandana, her skin, blue-white like powdered milk.

"What did they do to you?" He pulled the bandana away, the tug opening the wound again. He tossed the blood-soaked cloth into the bush, and then stripped off his Ramones shirt, ripped a length off the bottom and used it to tie the rest of the shirt around her arm. "You need to go to the hospital."

"I don't want to go to a hospital." Zoe felt four years old, small and helpless.

"You need stitches, Zoe."

"No hospital."

"I'll take you to the free clinic then, okay?"

"Okay." Zoe was so terribly, horribly, awfully tired. She just wanted to lie down, rest her head on her good arm and go to sleep. It was all over. The Beckoners were done. She'd survived. Roll the credits. Drop the curtain. Up the lights.

The nurse at the clinic gave Zoe thirty stitches and did not believe for one second that she had slashed herself, which is what Zoe told her. The nurse had Zoe draw an X with her left hand, the one she would've had to have used. She couldn't do it neatly, let alone with any control. The nurse pursed her lips and sewed Zoe up, all the while carrying on an elaborate conversation over her head with Leaf about asinine gang practices, the dangers of tetanus, and the stench of rotting gangrenous limbs.

"Sorry about your shirt, Leaf." Zoe sipped the apple juice the nurse gave her in the waiting room after, along with a packet of cookies the nurse said she had to eat before she was allowed to leave. The sugar would help her body work to replace the blood she'd lost. "It's ruined."

"Never mind that." He pushed a lock of hair away from her face and tucked it behind her ear. "I don't care about the shirt."

"You do so."

"Okay, so I do. I'll have a little cry later on in private, but hey, guess what? I've got good news for you."

"Brady's truck exploded and all the Beckoners died in a ball of flames?"

"No. The good news is that you still have your hair."

"Nah." Zoe fingered ends of her braids. "The good news is that it's finally, completely over. Let's go home and tell April."

Zoe and Leaf launched into their story before they even got their coats off, but April was in a hurry to leave.

"I have to go." She pulled on her coat. "The babies are asleep in Alice's bed." She pushed past Zoe to the door.

"Stop, April." Zoe grabbed her. "Don't you get it? It's over."

"That's great." April opened the door.

"That's it? I get thirty stitches for you and that's all you have to say?"

"I'll believe it when I see it," she said, and then she left.

Zoe and Leaf looked at each other, eyebrows raised, and then went upstairs to check on the kids.

by streetlight

Teo called the mess on Zoe's arm her beauty mark. Simon called it the alien probe site. Leaf did his best to avoid mentioning it, and April never talked about it at all. In fact, she wasn't talking to Zoe much at all those days. Neither was Alice, for that matter. How could Alice not notice something was wrong? Before Zoe got the stitches out, she'd walk around clutching her elbows to keep from picking at them, and yet Alice floated around the house like she lived there all by herself. This was a problem. The day after Zoe got her stitches out, she came home and found Cassy squatting on the counter beside the stove, all four elements glowing orange hot. Alice was in the living room talking on the phone.

"Mom!" Zoe whisked Cassy off the counter with her good arm and dumped her on the linoleum. Cassy started to cry.

"Hon, is that you?" Alice pulled the phone away from her ear and covered the mouthpiece with her hand. "Would you see what Cassy's crying about? I'm on the phone."

That's for sure. On the phone *all* the time. Zoe couldn't remember the last time her mother actually cooked a real meal, or cleaned the toilet bowl, or asked her how her day at school was, or if she was surviving at all or was slowly dying before her very own oblivious eyes.

Alice always kept emergency cash behind the phone bills in the file cabinet, and it was when Zoe went in there to help herself to some money to rent a movie that she noticed the amount of the last phone bill. It was triple what it should be. It was as much as they spent on groceries for an entire month.

They'd never had a phone bill for that much. Zoe wondered if Alice had skipped paying for a couple of months, so she looked back, but no, all the bills they'd received since they'd moved to Abbotsford, except for the first month, were all that much or more, and every single long distance call was to the same number in Whitehorse.

Zoe took the bills downstairs, perplexed. Leaf was at the table cutting a puppet stage out of a cardboard box for Connor and Cassy, who were playing on the floor, piling up blocks and knocking them down. Zoe showed him what she'd discovered.

"Classifieds." He sliced out a wide arch. "She's met someone. Probably on the Internet."

"My mother doesn't know how to use the Internet."

"Then a newspaper ad, unless it's some long lost relative or something."

"We don't have relatives. The only long lost relative is Kenneth, my father. He Who Shall Not Be Mentioned."

"An old boyfriend?"

"No. She's a staunch graduate from the love 'em and leave 'em school of dating."

"Someone new then." Leaf shrugged. "So what?"

"So what? Why won't she tell me about it? I'm down here making dinner and doing the laundry and practically raising her youngest child, and she's up there having phone sex with some bushman of the north?"

"Yeah." Leaf set the box on the floor. "That about sums it up."

After listening to her speculate all over the place for nearly a week, what if this and what if that, Simon finally clutched her shoulders and said through gritted teeth, "Just call the damn number and ask."

So Zoe did, but after the man said hello she'd chickened out and hung up. Maybe she didn't want to know that bad.

Zoe tried listening at Alice's bedroom door again, carefully setting the glass quietly against the door, but Alice heard. She managed not to hear when Cassy was screaming because Zoe was washing her dinosaur cup, but she could hear that?

"Scram." She snatched the glass and kicked the door shut with her foot.

The next day, Zoe had been talking about the bushman again, in the Dungeon after school with everybody there, even Teo. He was still April's official bodyguard, even though Zoe tried to convince him that it was all over. April had been quiet, typing away, and then she suddenly sighed, dropping her hands to her lap.

"Just ask her."

The others looked at Zoe, eyebrows raised.

"She tried that already," Simon said. "Her mom wouldn't tell her."

Zoe looked at her shoes.

"Well?" Simon said. "You've asked her, haven't you?"

"No," Zoe muttered.

"Why not?" Leaf asked.

Zoe was about to tell them why not, but soon realized she didn't have any good reason except for that's not how things worked in her family. Outright asking? Too easy?

The next day was Teo's birthday. Wish was making pizza for them all next door. The boys and April convinced Zoe to ask Alice while they were all there to make sure she did it. They trooped next door and everyone but Zoe slipped upstairs to wait in Zoe's room while she stayed downstairs to ask Alice, who for a change was not busting out of the house to go to an AA meeting. She was curled on the couch under an afghan, settling in to watch *I Love Lucy* on the channel that came in the least fuzzy.

Zoe plunked herself down on the other end of the couch and waited for a commercial break, as Alice was always testier if Zoe tried to talk to her when a show was on.

"So," Zoe hoped her voice sounded casual. "Who've you been talking to all the time, on the phone?"

"You think that's any of your business?" Alice's eyes were locked on the TV.

"Yes."

"What makes you think that, huh?"

"The fact that you might as well be on another planet." Zoe fought the urge to launch into an inventory of all the reasons that made it her business. "You have no idea what's going on around here."

"I don't, do I?"

"No, you don't."

"You could tell me anytime you felt like it."

"And you could maybe bother to ask."

Alice pushed aside the afghan and sat up.

"Can you guess?" She lit a cigarette and looked at Zoe, even though the show had come back on. "Come on, guess."

"I have no idea."

"None?" Alice smiled. "Sure you do, come on, take a guess."

"I don't want to guess, Mom. Just tell me."

"Harris."

"Harris Kellerman?"

Alice looked back at the TV. "He's the only Harris I know."

"You dumped him." Zoe thought back to when they left Prince George. "What does he want with you?"

"What do you think?" Alice made a great production of getting up and turning up the volume. "Do you mind?"

"Do I mind what?"

"I told you what you wanted to know. I'm watching this." Her eyes wandered up. "Don't you have guests upstairs? Or did they leave over the roof?"

"What the hell?"

"*What*?"

"What's up with you and Harris?"

"Look, Zoe," Alice stubbed out her cigarette. "We talk on the phone. That's all."

"That's all? Hours and hours a day and you say that's all? What's going on? Is he trying to get you back? Is that it?"

"You remember that night before we left? When he came over? He asked me to marry him."

"Since when did that mean anything?"

"He quit drinking."

"Again? How many times is this? As many as you? Huh?"

"Watch where you're going with that, missy."

"Where I'm not going with that is anywhere near Whitehorse." Zoe stood up. "Do you get that? There is no way I am moving to Whitehorse. Do you understand what I'm saying?"

"It's kind of hard to understand someone when they're acting like a spoilt little brat."

"Must be hard to understand yourself, then." Zoe turned to leave, but Alice grabbed her wrist.

"Don't you use that tone with me!" She wagged a finger at Zoe, her voice rising. "Just who the hell do you think you are talking to me like that? Harris is a kind, loving man who treats me right. You want me to turn away from that?"

"Then why did you make us leave?" Zoe yelled at her. In the pregnant pause that followed, she heard her friends moving around upstairs.

Alice went to the bottom of the stairs, hands on her hips, and called for them to come down.

"I think your friends should leave," she said as they filed passed, eyes on the floor.

"Well, I think they should stay." Behind her, the others were pulling on their jackets.

"We'll be at my house," Leaf mumbled, holding open the door. "Bye, Alice."

"Uh-huh." Alice fixed her eyes on Zoe and waited for Leaf to shut the door behind him. "I suggest you take a minute to think before you open that big fat mouth of yours again."

"Is that a suggestion from one of your precious self-help tapes?"

"You better—"

"I'm not moving to Whitehorse."

"I'm not deaf."

"Nobody is moving to Whitehorse."

"Oh yeah? And just who is it that makes the decisions around here?"

"You, and they all suck!"

Alice reached out and smacked Zoe across the face so hard that Zoe reeled back and knocked into the wall.

"You're grounded, young lady!"

"Right, nice try." Zoe walked out and slammed the door behind her.

"Fine then, never mind being grounded!" Alice flung open the door and hollered from the stoop. "Don't even think of coming back here until you are good and ready to apologize!"

Wish and the others were waiting for her next door. It was muffled, but they could all hear Alice ranting through the walls, swearing up a storm. Zoe heard Cassy wailing for her and decided to go get her. She pounded on the door, but Alice had locked it and was ignoring her. Zoe thought she'd outsmart her by going over the roof, but Alice had already thought to lock Zoe's window. Zoe stood outside on the carport roof in the rain, looking in at Cassy, who had her face pressed to the window, crying for her.

"Go find mama," Zoe told her, giving up. She waited until Cassy toddled out of the room, sobbing, and then she crossed back over to Leaf's.

Later, after the others left and Wish and T-Bone had gone up to bed, Zoe and Leaf crawled under the covers of his narrow single bed and turned off the light. The two of them had to spoon tight so neither of them would fall off. They fell asleep like that. Zoe woke in the middle of the night and when she turned to stretch her cramped legs, Leaf woke too, and in the silent still night, the streetlight illuminating their faces, they pulled off each other's clothes.

"Whoa, hang on." Leaf twisted away. "I don't have any condoms."

"Who said we were going that far?"

"We're not?" Leaf kneeled over her.

"No."

"Soon?" He kissed her nipple.

Zoe closed her eyes. She wanted to. If he kissed her there again, it might be sooner than she planned. "Yeah. I think very soon."

Leaf rolled onto his back. After a minute, he said, "I have an idea."

"What?" Zoe wasn't sure what she could handle at this point.

"Let's make it sound like we're doing it, and then in the morning we'll see what kind of lecture Wish'll think up."

The two of them bounced and groaned dramatically, breaking into giggles at the sound of the bedsprings creaking like something out of a B-movie.

In the morning, Wish brought them breakfast in bed: eggs and toast and frothy lattes in deep bowls. Either Wish and T-Bone had slept right though the racket, or they weren't going to bother with any lecture. Not at this point anyway.

In the light of day, the idea of apologizing to her mother didn't seem so bad. To be honest, Zoe figured she had reason to thank her mother. If they hadn't had that fight, Zoe would not have ended up in Leaf's bed. There was no way Alice would've *let* her spend the night with Leaf.

Alice took her sweet time answering the door.

"You forget something?"

"I'm sorry, Mom." Zoe tried not to sound as happy as she felt.

Alice crossed her arms and let several seconds pass. "You're sorry."

"Yeah."

"Well, come on in, then." Alice disappeared inside. "I'll boil a teabag for that bruise on your face."

Zoe had felt so great when she woke up that she hadn't noticed the purple welt announcing where Alice had ploughed her the night before. Zoe looked at her reflection in the hallway mirror. She put a fingertip to her puffy cheek, and then she pulled up her sleeve to get the whole effect: swollen eye, bruised cheek and demolished wreck of an arm. She looked awful, but she had to admit that she had never felt better in her whole life.

warm fuzzies

And they all lived happily ever after, nowhere near Whitehorse. The end.

Only not quite. The real end, if there's ever an end to anything, began on the last day of school before the Christmas holidays. The weather nagged at Zoe like a snot-nosed kid pulling on her arm. The sky was bruised and heavy and low, and it hadn't stopped raining for weeks. Zoe missed snow for the first time. She missed making snow angels and the way her nose hairs froze when she breathed in the cold, dry, northern air. Snow made everything clean and quiet and right. All this rain, it was as if April's God was trying to wash away some awful stain that just would not come out.

Zoe pulled the covers over her head. Just one more day until the holidays, one more day until she could stay in her pajamas and watch movies all day if she wanted to. She trudged up to the school and headed straight for the Dungeon. Leaf wasn't there, but the Christmas issue of the paper was, five tall stacks just outside the door, bound with flat plastic ties. Zoe cut the ties and sent the papers off via the Creative Writing geeks who had a monthly spread in the paper in exchange for delivering them around the school. She kept three papers aside, one for her, one for Leaf and one for April. She unlocked the Dungeon and put their copies on their desks, and then flopped on the couch to look through it. Usually all she looked for was layout errors, but something else stuck out that day. Page two had been rearranged to include another piece. The headline read, "What Would You Do?" As Zoe read the piece, a wave of nausea rose up in her belly.

What Would You Do?

What would you do if you saw someone being raped? This is the first question in what will become a weekly poll. Read the scenario, and then choose the answer that best applies to you. Cut out the answer ballot and drop it in the box outside the Dungeon.

We want to keep the answers confidential, so don't put your name on it. But while you're here, fill out our "WWYD" contest ballots. You could win two free movie passes. If you have a scenario you'd like to see in the *Reporter*, drop it off, in writing, to April Donnelly—assistant editor.

SCENARIO #1:

You're at the first big party of the year, in fact, it's your first big party ever.
After wishing the drunk birthday girl "Happy Birthday" and being embarrassed by her and her cronies in the kitchen, you go out onto the patio for a bit of fresh air. But as you walk through the yard, you hear a muffled cry come from the bushes. It's a new friend of yours, a small, thin member of the tough in-crowd, and that's not her boyfriend with her. It's another girl's boyfriend. At first you think you've stumbled onto some kind of love triangle, but the girl's cries of protest make you realize that she is the victim of unconsentual sex. She's being raped, and you're a witness. What do you do?

a) Interrupt and take the girl to safety
b) Run and call the police
c) Go inside and get help
d) Nothing

Don't forget to bring your ballots to the Dungeon for your chance to win!

April had read Zoe's diary.

How could she? After everything, how *could* she? It had to have been the night she babysat Cassy and Connor at Zoe's, the night Zoe lay bleeding to death in the parking lot, knifed, for god's sake, and all the while April was rooting through her stuff and doing to Zoe the exact same thing the Beckoners had done to her.

The realization that April had read Zoe's diary was worse than getting thirty stitches, worse than being slashed. This felt like being ripped wide open, head to toe. And here it was for everyone to see, on page two of the Christmas issue, the most widely read issue of the year—practically the only issue read all year—because of the three pages of seasonal warm fuzzies at the back. People who never picked up the paper read this issue, and there was another entire population that thought the paper only *had* one issue—the Christmas issue. And worse, by far the worst of all, was that all it would take would be one Beckoner to look at it and they'd know exactly what and who it was about.

Zoe put her head in her hands. She would have to stay in the Dungeon until everyone had left for the day. She'd have to wait until the janitor came by to lock up, and then maybe he could escort her home if she pleaded hard enough, if she begged for her life. She'd have to change schools now, maybe even bus to the next district.

Leaf came in then, three more copies of the paper under his arm.

"Beat me to it." He kissed her on the cheek. "What do you think? We could use a little hype, huh? The movie pass was my idea."

Zoe stared at the ballot, at D in particular—the one she had chosen. April reading her diary, that was bad enough, but Zoe's guilt was worse than bad. It was paralyzing. She was a big fat D. D for nothing. D for failed. D for doghouse, doomed, dead, demolished, destroyed.

"What are you trying to prove?" She forced the words through trembling lips.

"What do you mean?"

"This!" She pushed the paper onto the floor. "What the hell is this?"

"It was April's idea."

"I bet it was." Zoe shook her head. "You have no idea what you've done, do you?"

"Obviously not. Why don't you tell me?"

Zoe grabbed her pack and stood up.

"Zoe, tell me what this is about."

"I need to find April."

Leaf grabbed her arm. "Zoe, don't go like this."

"Don't touch me!" She yanked her arm away and slammed out of the Dungeon. The hallway seemed overly bright, the Christmas decorations garish and cheap, the carols piped through the PA system suddenly cloying. There was nowhere to go. There was no point in hiding. Even at a school in another district they'd find her sooner or later.

The newspaper was everywhere. Zoe made her way across the school, barely resisting the urge to rip the paper out of people's hands as she passed. She wished she had telekinetic powers and could set the papers ablaze just by looking at them.

She finally spotted April outside the main entrance, waiting in line to pass through the security station. Zoe glared at her. When April had cleared the metal detector, she hesitated, evaluating Zoe's expression. Zoe had no words yet, but she grabbed April's sleeve, dragged her across the hall and into the girls' bathroom. When she let go, April backed up against the sink and covered her face with her hands.

"I'm not going to hit you," Zoe hissed. "But I can't think of what I can say to you that would make you understand what you've done."

April said nothing for a long second. "They won't know how I found out."

"They will, April. Why did you do it?"

"To get back at them."

"They were finally leaving us alone, don't you get that? You just gave them the reason they've been waiting for to start again."

"Why didn't you help Jazz? Were you afraid of them? Is that why you just left her there?"

"You should know. You read my diary."

"But how could you just walk away from her? What if it was you? What if—"

"What if I say that you will never live this down? *I* will never live this down. You thought last year was bad? You just wait.

Once the Beckoners read it everyone will know exactly who you were writing about, and everyone will know that you found out from me."

"This isn't about you, Zoe. No one will know how I found out."

"No one will believe me if I say I didn't tell you anything. No one will believe me that you just *happened* to find out. They'll think I told you."

"Maybe not."

"Are you that stupid?"

"I didn't mean to get you in trouble, Zoe. I just wanted to get back at the Beckoners. Once and for all."

"I don't care what you *did* or *didn't* mean to do. You *did* it. And now we are both screwed. Do you even get that? What it means to be screwed?"

"Ask Jazz." April's expression darkened. "Besides, what have I got to lose?"

"Absolutely nothing, because you are a nothing. And do you know why? Because you are a professional loser. You will always be a loser, and even worse, you're the kind of loser that people go out of their way to hate, because just you breathing pushes people's buttons." Zoe slapped her copy of the paper hard onto the counter, expecting April to flinch, but she didn't. She held her ground in an aggravating self-righteous way. "You know what, though? Even though it sucks to be me right now, I am so glad I am not you. You are in so deep, April. You have no idea."

April shook her head in disbelief. "And you still have no idea how wrong it was to not do anything that night, do you?"

"You read what I wrote, April." A lump in Zoe's throat made it suddenly hard to swallow. "How do you think I felt?"

All traces of April's apprehension were gone. "Not bad enough to do anything about it."

"You're dead," Zoe whispered. "I'd disappear if I were you. When the Beckoners come for you this time, it won't be to lynch some plastic mannequin."

"Like I don't already know that." April pushed past Zoe and out into the crowded hallway.

The average incubation time for big-ticket gossip is about three periods, which put Zoe and her chaos in the middle of the cafeteria at noon. She'd managed to avoid the Beckoners all morning and had decided to spend the lunch hour in the cafeteria because that was the last place they'd be caught dead in, especially because the Rejoice In His Name youth group were throwing a birthday party for Jesus, complete with cake and balloons.

The Beckoners were lurking though; she'd heard people mention them in hushed and not so hushed conversations all morning. Word was getting around.

Leaf cut into the food line ahead of Zoe.

"You have to tell me what's going on." He gripped her shoulders. "This is not good. The whole thing really happened? I printed something true?"

"You could make it a little worse by forcing me to explain myself here."

"Sorry." He put two plates of fries on her tray and took it from her. He added two iced teas, and then pushed it along to the cashier. "My treat," he said. "By the sounds of it, this might be your last meal."

"It's the least you could do."

They headed to a table in the corner by the fire escape, as far away from the Jesus freaks as possible. By the looks and jeers, it was obvious people knew it was Zoe in the scenario. People sang in a schoolyard lilt, "*What would you do, Zoe?*" as they passed.

"The Beckoners are looking for you and Dog," some girl Zoe had never even seen before hollered across the wide room. "I'd watch my back if I was you." Zoe stopped in her tracks, marveling in the sudden urge to beat up the girl. She'd never had that feeling before. She clenched her fists.

"Ignore them." Leaf nudged her with the tray. "Keep walking."

Zoe kept her fists clenched and her eyes forward until they reached the table. Leaf put down the tray and took her hands.

"I didn't know. I'm sorry. She brought it in last night after you left, and I thought it was a great idea. I put it in just before it left for the printers. I'm so sorry."

"There's nothing you can do about it now. There's no use apologizing."

"I'll print a retraction. I'll do an editorial in the next issue."

"It won't do any good." Zoe stared at her fries. "It's all going to blow."

"Will you tell me what happened?"

"What have you heard?"

"That it was Brady, and most people think the girl is Jazz, but no one's exactly sure."

Zoe covered her face with her hands. "I don't believe this is happening."

"You saw it all?"

She nodded. "I have to get out of here."

"It'll blow over. By the time the holidays are over, no one will care."

"I'm not worried about 'no one,' I'm worried about the Beckoners."

"They said they'd leave you alone, though. Those stitches were your ticket out."

"You believe that?" Zoe looked up. "They'll think this gives them the right to do whatever the hell they want with me, Leaf."

"I'm just trying to help, Zoe. What can I say?"

"There's nothing to say."

An awkward silence settled between them. Zoe felt like all the clocks in the world had slowed down to a painfully slow crawl. Each second carved a year out of her life. This day would never end. It would just loop itself over and over. In the far corner, the Jesus freaks were singing a pop version of "Happy Birthday," clapping and drumming on the tables.

"Do you want to tell me your side of the story?" Leaf asked over the din.

Zoe shook her head.

"The whole school has just the one version, Zoe. Why don't you get your side of the story out there? It might help."

"No."

"Why not?"

"Because I'm not a rat."

"Everyone's going to know by the end of the day anyway, you've said so yourself. What's the difference if you tell now?"

"I never told anyone anything. That's the way I thought she wanted it. I'm not going to start spreading rumors now." Zoe stabbed at her fries with her fork. "That's the difference."

"Will you at least tell me how April found out? Did you tell her?"

"Why don't you ask her?" Zoe stabbed the fries harder. "Seeing as you two were both in on it."

"I wasn't *in* on anything. I had no idea." Leaf took her fork away. "I swear I didn't know. I thought it was all made up. I thought it was just a scenario. I thought it'd be a great way to get more people to read the paper, you know?" He took one of her hands in both of his. "Tell me what happened, Zoe."

"You won't tell anyone?"

He kissed the back of her hand. "Never."

"Okay." Zoe took a deep breath and let it out slowly with the first words. "It was at Beck's birthday. I saw Jazz and Brady and freaked. I ran down the mountain and then Simon and Teo saw me and took me home. I was a mess. I went home and I wrote about it in my diary and April read it. The end."

"So it was Jazz," Leaf murmured.

Zoe covered her face with her hands again. "I didn't mean to say her name."

There was a commotion in the far corner. A large chunk of the Jesus birthday cake flew across the room. Zoe looked up and saw the top of Beck's head.

"Where is she?" Beck hollered. "Zoe? If you're in here you better run for it because you are dead, bitch!"

Beck stormed down the middle of the cafeteria, dragging April behind her. The rest of the Beckoners and a posse of Brady's friends were close behind, all of them eating a piece of birthday cake. Beck pointed at Zoe. "On second thought, don't move!"

Jazz brought up the rear, clutching herself and staring at the linoleum as she dragged her feet. Heather stopped mid-stride and spun on her heel.

"Hurry your ass, *Jasvinder*."

"We're leaving." Leaf kicked a chair out of the way and stationed himself between the Beckoners and Zoe. "Let's go." He took her hand and pulled her towards the fire exit, but Trevor blocked their way, flanked by two enormous I'll-do-anything-for-free-weed zombies Zoe had never seen before.

"You're not going anywhere." A dollop of icing stuck on Trevor's chin. He stuck his tongue way out to lick it off.

Heather flounced up and jabbed Zoe in the chest. "Dog says she read about my party in your diary. But you know what? I don't believe her. I think you told her."

"She didn't." April gasped between sobs, cheeks blotchy and red. "She didn't tell me anything!"

"Shut up, bitch." Beck shoved April onto her knees.

"Did you tell her?" Heather leaned forward. "Or did she read it in your little diary?"

"I didn't tell her anything. I didn't tell anyone."

"See? I told you, Heather," Janika said. "I said she never told, didn't I?" She turned to Lindsay for confirmation. Lindsay ignored her.

"This is ridiculous." Leaf's grip on Zoe's hand tightened. "Do you people always act like you've had frontal lobotomies?"

"Stay out of this, tree boy."

"Gladly, and I'll take Zoe and April with me. If you'll excuse us..." Leaf tried to push past Trevor, but Brady grabbed a hold of Leaf's collar and held him back.

"You're not going anywhere, asshole."

Leaf held out his hand and smiled a used-car-salesman grin. "And you'd be the rapist?"

Brady let go of Leaf, balled his fist and ploughed Leaf in the face with such force that it knocked him over. Trevor stepped neatly to the side so Leaf would hit the floor when he fell. Leaf groaned, eyes squeezed shut.

"Leaf!" Zoe knelt beside him.

Lindsay towered over them with the iced teas. "You should ice that." She dumped the ice tea onto them. Laughter cut through the spectators who'd gathered. Everyone closed in, like they'd all taken one giant step closer. All Zoe could see was a thick border of legs and torsos blocking the exit and cheering on the Beckoners.

"Ask Jazz!" April screamed, struggling to get up. Beck and Lindsay held her down, boots on her back. "Ask *her* why she's still a Beckoner! She's the one Brady raped!"

Jazz's dark eyes went as wide as pucks. The word "rape" rippled through the crowd disapprovingly, as though they were watching a hockey game and the away team had just scored.

"Shut up, April." Zoe wiped her face with the bottom of her shirt. "Just shut up."

"But it's not true!" Heather shouted at the crowd. "Don't you get it? Zoe made it up! It never really happened!"

"I didn't make it up." It took all of Zoe's will not to look at Jazz. "It happened."

"And what does that say about me, huh?" Brady loomed over her, rage dripping off him like sweat.

Zoe looked around, at the crowd hanging on her next words, at Heather, who stared hard at Jazz. Brady's scowl quivered.

Zoe took a deep breath. "Do you really want me to get into that here?"

"Zoe!" Simon called, following Teo, who was pushing their way through the crowd. "Leaf! Are you okay?"

"No," Leaf mumbled.

Teo took one look at Leaf on the floor. He grabbed Brady by his collar.

"Did you do that? Huh?" Teo shook him. "Did you hit him?"

"Don't touch me, you faggot!" Brady struggled to get away. "Get him off me!"

Brady's friends surged forward.

"Fight! Fight!" the crowd chanted. "Fight! Fight!"

Teo let go of Brady. As Brady set himself up to punch Teo, Teo hooked the back of Brady's leg with his foot. Brady fell over backward. As Trevor grabbed one of Teo's arms, and one of his cronies grabbed the other, Teo strained forward, landing three hard kicks to Brady's side. Brady struggled onto his knees, and then stood, obviously in pain.

"Oh my God!" Simon climbed onto a table. "Help!" He waved both his arms frantically, as Brady took a moment to recover before starting in on Teo, who was being restrained.

"OKAY, break it up!" Cromwell's voice sliced the taut silence.

The crowd booed in disappointment, and reluctantly split to let him through. Cromwell hurried forward, two security guards following him.

"What exactly is going on here?"

"Nothing, Cromwell." Beck flashed him her princess-of-everything smile. Heather draped an arm over his shoulder and batted her eyes. He pushed her away and nodded at Leaf, whose nose was bloody, his eye swelling shut.

"What happened to you?"

"I fell."

"Tell me something I'll believe." Cromwell turned to the security guards. "Clear this place out. I want it empty. You," he nodded at April, still huddled on the floor in tears. "What's the matter with you?"

"She tripped," Lindsay said.

Cromwell whipped a finger at her. "I wasn't talking to you." He pulled a balled-up tissue from his sports jacket and handed it to April. "Get up. Clean yourself up and wait for me in my office."

"Oooo," someone way back in the safety of the crowd sang, "April and Cromwell, sittin' in a tree..."

"ENOUGH!" Cromwell's face went a hot red. He held out a hand to April. "Get up." April took his hand and struggled to her feet.

Cromwell got busy directing three more security guards who'd arrived.

"Hey, Dog, hang on," Beck said. "I got something for you." She smacked the back of April's head with a rolled up copy of the paper. "Bad dog," she whispered. "Bad dog." She hit her with the paper one more time, before Cromwell turned his attention back to the Beckoners. Beck handed the paper to April.

"Beck, you and your little savages are going straight to Mr. Seaton's office, accompanied by Officer Tucker here." He sent them off with a guard fretting at their heels like a border collie. "And you two," he wagged a finger at Zoe and Leaf, "the two of you get out of my sight before I change my mind about letting you go."

in the park

Harris showed up the next day, unannounced. Zoe knew it was him when he was still two blocks away. His truck had gotten worse. It was a miracle he'd made it all the way down from Whitehorse without it dying along the way. Zoe watched from her window as Alice ran, in her bare feet, through the icy rain to the truck. She leapt into his arms, covering his face with kisses.

"You're not moving in, are you?" Zoe sat on the bottom stair and watched him lug in two big suitcases.

Alice eyed her severely from the door.

"Nice to see you too, kid." Harris opened his arms. Zoe stayed where she was. Cassy ran to him. Zoe couldn't help but feel betrayed. Harris swept her up and onto his shoulders. He kicked one of the suitcases. "And by the way, my crap's in the truck. These are full of presents."

From that point on, Zoe spent most of her time next door. This accomplished two things: avoiding Alice and Harris's happy little family act and avoiding the Beckoners. It was strange, not having the Dungeon to go to. They were all so used to the tiny room that even though Wish told them more than once that it was okay to come downstairs, Simon and Teo and Leaf and Zoe pretty much stayed in Leaf's room. April was not there.

That afternoon after the mess in the cafeteria, while she boiled and cooled teabags to put on Leaf's black eye, Zoe had sworn that she would never speak to April again. April had phoned at least once every day, and the guys had all tried to change Zoe's mind, but as far as Zoe was concerned, April had burned whatever creaky, rotting, carpenter ant infested bridge there had ever been between them.

The next time Zoe saw April was in the mall on Christmas Eve. Zoe finally had to admit that Harris was not going to leave anytime soon, so she went out to buy him a present, leaving him and Alice happily bumping around the tiny kitchen, cooking and baking for that night's dinner at Fraser House. Alice twisted out of Harris's embrace as Zoe left.

"Be back before six, hon."

"Yeah." Zoe rolled her eyes as Harris began nibbling Alice's neck.

"I mean it," Alice said. "Dinner's at seven."

Zoe had truly believed that the mall would be deserted except for a few last minute shoppers. On the contrary, it was crawling with crazed consumer lunatics fighting over the last this or that like it was food and they hadn't eaten in weeks. Zoe wondered how many of the dozen or so violent spats she witnessed involved self-proclaimed peace-loving Christians.

After over an hour of pushing her way through the crowds, Zoe just needed to sit down for a minute. She headed for the washroom on the upper level. Normally it was empty, but that day there was a lineup out the door of haggard mothers wrestling with squalling babies and red-faced toddlers. The two chairs just inside the door were both occupied by limp old ladies. Zoe joined the line and ended up sitting on a toilet until the bathroom slowly began to empty. At long last there was perfect silence, except for the Christmas carols piping in through tinny speakers in the ceiling.

The bathroom wasn't entirely empty, though. Zoe spied the familiar yellow canvas shoes first. It was April, slumped in one of the chairs by the door, a heap of shopping bags and packages on the chair beside her. When April saw her come out of the stall, she got up to leave. Zoe was too tired to be angry at that moment. She went to the sink and washed her hands, waiting for April to leave first.

April was halfway out the door, and then she paused.

"I'm really sorry, Zoe."

Zoe ignored her.

"I'm sorry," April said again.

"I heard you the first time." Zoe dried her hands and put the paper towel in the garbage. "Where'd you go on Friday?"

"Cromwell sent me home."

"Oh. Same with us."

April sat down again. "You're still mad at me?"

"Of course I am."

"Are you going to stay mad?"

"That's my plan." Zoe wanted to leave, but she found herself sitting beside April instead and saying, "You should never have read my diary. That wasn't right."

April sighed. "We could go in circles with this. What you did wasn't right either." She tightened her grip on her bags and stood up again.

"Wait," Zoe said. "Maybe I didn't do the right thing, but a lot of people would've done the same thing in my place."

"That doesn't make it right."

"It might not, but still, what happened at Beck's birthday has nothing to do with what happened in the cafeteria. What I did or didn't do did not cause that."

"No, it didn't." April stared at her feet. "I'm sorry about the scenario. It was a stupid idea. I wasn't thinking about you at all. I just wanted to get back at the Beckoners. I screwed up."

"You sure did."

"How's Leaf? He looked terrible."

"He's okay. There's hardly a bruise anymore. It'll make a good story some day."

"What we go through for a story, huh?"

"You're telling me." Zoe rehearsed the next words in her head several times before saying them out loud. "I owe you an apology."

"What for?" April looked surprised.

"For the Beckoners. For everything. For treating you so bad."

"You're not that bad."

"But I have been."

"Yeah. You have."

"You know what's strange?" Zoe looked at April. "If I hadn't met Beck first...if things had happened in a different order...we might've been friends right from the beginning."

"I don't know about that," April said.

"I think it's true." Zoe stood up. "You on your way home?"

April nodded.

"I've still got to find something for Harris."

"He's here?"

"Yeah," Zoe said. She began telling April all about the lovebirds as they left together out the rear doors, where Shadow was waiting for April.

The night was cold and dry for the first time in ages. It even smelled like it might snow. Christmas carols whined out from speakers in the parking lot. The girls crossed to the back corner, which had been sectioned off to sell Christmas trees. The trail through Mill Lake, the short cut home, branched off from there. There weren't many Christmas trees left, just a few scraggly ones, and a couple too big for even Heather's cathedral living room. An old man in an orange parka was rolling up the plastic fencing. He waved and wished them Merry Christmas as they passed.

They walked in silence through the dark stand of pines to the clearing at the top of the park. A Muzak version of "What Child is This?" carried on the wind from the parking lot. April hummed along, out of tune. The deserted park spread out below them, the lake at the center, a halo of ice around the edge reflecting the moonlight. Their breath puffed out like smoke as they headed down the knoll, stepping sideways so they wouldn't lose their footing on the icy grass.

Halfway across the park April stopped.

"Oh, no. *Look.*"

Zoe strained to see what April was looking at in the misty dark. The Beckoners filed silently out from the bandstand, where they'd been waiting in the shadows. They formed a line across the path, blocking the way, except for Jazz, who lingered off to the side.

"What do we do, Zoe?"

"Go back to the Christmas tree guy," Zoe whispered.

"We weren't expecting to see you, Zoe." Beck took a drag off her cigarette and then chucked the butt at Zoe.

"Let us go, Beck."

"Can't do that." She shook her head. "Sorry."

"Then let April go."

"Ah, but Dog is the one we have the problem with. Several problems," Beck said. "You can go. We're done with you. You've got the scars to know better than to piss us off again. Apparently, after all this time, Dog hasn't learned her lesson yet."

Tears streamed down April's face. "Go," she whispered to Zoe.

"I'll get help," Zoe whispered.

"That would just make it worse," April whispered back.

"What have we got here?" Lindsay grabbed April's shopping bags. She pulled out a toy car racetrack and handed it to Heather. "Merry Christmas, Malcolm." One by one she pulled out April's presents and re-distributed them. When she was done, she balled up the empty shopping bags and chucked them at April.

"You can't do this," Zoe said. "This isn't fair. Give the presents back."

"Or what?" Lindsay said. "You'll take them back?"

"Give them back. This isn't funny."

"Whoever said any of this was *funny*?" Heather said. "Do you think it's *funny* to call my boyfriend a rapist? Do you think that's *funny*?"

"If the name fits," Zoe muttered, unable to stop herself.

"Now, see? There you go." Beck clucked her tongue. "It's shit like that that gets you into trouble in the first place. Isn't that right, Brady?"

"Uh-huh," he growled. "You have no idea how much trouble." A vein in his neck throbbed visibly. "You have no idea what I could do to you."

"Oh, but I do," Zoe said. "That's just it, Brady. I know *exactly* what you can do. It's no lie. It's not some made-up story. I was there. I saw what you did to Jazz."

"You're lying!" Brady came at her with his fists up. Shadow's hackles rose. He lowered his head and growled.

"Go ahead! Hit me!" Zoe dropped to her knees and covered her face, waiting for the first blow. "Beat the shit out of me so I'll have bruises for proof! I'll go straight to the cops!"

"Wait!" Janika pushed Brady back. "Just hold on. Beck said you could go, Zoe. Why are you making it worse? Why don't you go? Just leave."

"I'm not leaving without April."

"That's not going to happen," Beck said. "Dog is ours."

"This is about getting even." Heather threw her shoulders back. "Dog isn't going anywhere until we're finished with her."

"Go, Zoe," April begged. "Please, take Shadow and just go."

"See?" Janika helped Zoe up. "Even *she* wants you to go. Just get out of here before it's too late."

Beck pulled out another cigarette. She lit it with her eight ball matches, casually, as though they were all just waiting in line to get into the movies. The Beckoners all glared at Zoe, a silent order for her to leave. She stood her ground. She was not going to leave without April.

All of a sudden, April spun around. She grabbed Zoe's hand, pulling her back. "Run!"

Zoe dropped her bags and stumbled after her. The two of them raced across the icy grass, Shadow straining to keep up with them. Lindsay, Beck, Heather, Brady and Trevor chased after them. Zoe looked back at one point; Beck and Brady were closing in.

"Faster!" she yelled.

April was almost at the top of the knoll. They were so close, Zoe could hear the Christmas carols again.

Then April slipped. Shadow caught up to her. Zoe flung herself between April and the others, but as April tried to get up, Beck and Brady shoved Zoe aside and grabbed onto April's legs.

"Let go of her!"

Shadow clamped down on Beck's leg. Brady kicked him so hard the dog landed three feet away.

"Don't hurt him!" April screamed. "Shadow, go home!"

He crept towards her, tail between his legs.

"Go HOME!" He kept coming. "GO HOME *NOW*!" He stopped, and then reluctantly turned and slunk off through the trees, looking back several times as Lindsay and Trevor caught up and held Zoe back.

When Shadow had disappeared, Beck and Brady dragged April down the slope by her feet. Heather led the way, head high, shoulders back like she was leading a royal procession. April folded her arms over her face and was still, like she'd given up.

"Help!" Zoe screamed, hoping the Christmas tree man would hear. "Help!" She tried to scramble up the hill, but Trevor and Lindsay's grip was solid.

Lindsay clamped her hand over Zoe's mouth and snarled in her ear, "You make one more sound and I will break your fingers, one by one."

She and Trevor forced Zoe down the hill, grasping her arms so tight she could feel their fingertips bruising her. Ahead of them, Beck and Brady dragged April on her back along the gravel path and up the steps of the bandstand, her head bumping against the wood. They dumped her in the middle of the wooden floor and stood back. April lifted herself onto her hands and knees.

"Don't bother." Beck kicked her back down.

Lindsay and Trevor pushed Zoe into a corner and stood on either side.

"Beck, let Zoe go." Janika put a shaky hand on Beck's shoulder. "You said she could go."

Beck slapped her hand away. "Maybe I changed my mind."

"Come on, Beck, she's just some small town hick who doesn't know what she's got herself into here. You wanted Dog; you've got her. Zoe just messes things."

"Let her go, Beck." Jazz spoke, for the first time since they'd met them on the path. "It's not her fault."

Beck glanced from Zoe to April to Heather to Jazz. She took one more pull on her cigarette, inhaled deeply and let her breath out slow. She grasped April's hair and yanked her head up with a snap.

"Hold her arms back, Lindsay."

April mewled as Lindsay pulled her arms away from her face.

"If I let you go, Zoe, you have to promise me one thing." Beck held the smoldering cigarette above April's face. "Promise me you'll shut up about this. We already know you have trouble keeping secrets. Maybe a warning will help you keep your mouth shut this time."

"Please, Beck." Zoe tried to step forward but the second she moved Trevor tightened his grip even more. "I'll do whatever you want, just don't hurt her."

"I want you to forget about tonight. I want you to forget about everything." She lowered the cigarette to barely an inch above April's forehead. "Because, believe me, I can make life difficult for you. And for Cassy too, if it comes to that."

Zoe wanted to tear her throat out then. Cassy's name should not be able to come out of Beck's mouth like that, so easily, so smooth, like she had as much right to say her name as Zoe did. Zoe wanted to rip out Beck's vocal cords and tie them in a knot so she'd never be able to say Cassy's name again. Before Zoe could take another breath, Beck lowered the cigarette again. Zoe couldn't take her eyes off it, though she desperately wanted to.

April kept her eyes open, until Beck finally touched the burning cigarette to her forehead. Then she gasped, screwing her eyes into tiny pinches, tears streaming down her cheeks.

There was no smell. Maybe the soft, icy wind carried it away. Maybe it was the wind that took away April's voice too, because through it all she was silent. Beck ground the cigarette into the burn and then pulled it away. The burn smoked like a gunshot wound.

"Open your eyes, bitch."

April didn't respond. Beck kicked her in the side. "Open your eyes and look at me or I'll do it again. I have a whole pack of these."

April opened her eyes halfway.

"I'm going to keep this little souvenir," Beck said. April shut her eyes again. Beck let go of her hair with a shove. Then she walked over to Zoe, holding the butt between her thumb and forefinger.

"Cassy…that magic word will keep you quiet, right?" She waved the butt in Zoe's face. "You tell anyone about tonight and I will come for her." She put the cigarette butt in her stash tin. "Keep that in mind. Keep Cassy in mind."

"Are you finished?" Janika said, barely keeping the edge out of her voice.

"With Zoe?" Beck looked Zoe up and down. "I'm finished with her. She can go."

Zoe tried to pull away from Trevor, but he tightened his grip. "She'll tell, Beck."

"She wouldn't dare, not now." Beck came up to her, face to face. "Would you?" She shoved Zoe hard in the chest. "You know enough not to tell, don't you, Zoe? Tell me you know that much."

Zoe nodded.

"Say it. Say, 'I promise not to tell.'"

"I promise not to tell," Zoe whispered.

"There's my girl." Beck patted her shoulder. "Trevor and Janika are going to go with you, to make sure you go straight home and keep your mouth shut." Beck reached out and tapped Zoe's lips with the same finger that had held the cigarette butt. She smelled of smoke, but a weird smoke that Zoe assumed was the smell of burning flesh. Her stomach flipped. Beck tapped Zoe's lips once for each word. "You won't say a word to anyone, will you?"

Zoe shook her head.

Two more taps. "Good girl."

Then Janika was on the other side of her, pulling her across the bandstand and down the stairs. Zoe looked back from the bottom step. From there she was eye-to-eye with April, still curled on the floor in the middle of the bandstand. She looked up, the burn in the middle of her forehead staring out like a third eye. She looked at Zoe for a second. Then she closed her eyes and laid her head down gently, like she was going to sleep.

Janika collected Zoe's shopping bags and pulled her along for a while. She was gentle. Trevor was not. He pushed Janika aside and shoved Zoe ahead of them like she was a prisoner of war, only she was getting away. She was free, and it felt awful. She didn't want to leave. She wanted to stay.

The three of them stopped at the edge of the park, as though once they stepped onto the sidewalk, they would cement something awful. Cars passed, full of families heading to Christmas all over town. A station wagon of Santas slowed to a stop at the curb. The Santa in the passenger seat rolled down his window and held out a fistful of little candy canes.

"Don't look so glum. It can't be that bad." His breath was rum and eggnog. "Ho, ho, ho, Merry Christmas, yadda, yadda, yadda."

Janika took the candy canes and the Santas drove off, honking their horn, the car hugging a little too close to the centerline. Zoe and Trevor and Janika stood there a moment longer, until from behind them in the park came one long scream that cut the night like a knife slicing silk. Then, they ran without stopping until they'd reached the empty lot behind Paradise Heights, the three of them gasping for breath.

"I'm going back," Trevor said. "You can babysit her." He started jogging back towards the lake.

Janika escorted Zoe to her door and handed her the shopping bags.

"Don't take this personally. It's just business."

All Zoe could do was shake her head.

"This goes on all the time, Zoe. It's just settling scores, you know?"

Zoe shook her head again.

"It's obvious you were never one of us." Janika sighed. "But you figured that out pretty quick, didn't you?"

Zoe nodded.

"You won't say anything, right?"

"What are you going to do to her?"

"We're just going to scare her, teach her a lesson." Janika backed down the driveway. "You won't say anything, right? I mean, I don't really have to stay here and babysit you, do I?"

Zoe shook her head again.

"I'm going to head back." Janika gestured back to the park. "Merry Christmas?"

Zoe shook her head once more.

shadow

Alice ripped into her for being late the minute that Zoe walked in the door.

"I told you to be back here by six and now it's six thirty and you—"

"Mom, listen to me—"

"I don't think so, missy." Alice handed her a mincemeat pie. "You better—"

"Mom!" Zoe shouted. "Listen to me!"

"No, *you* listen to *me*!"

Zoe hurled the pie against the wall.

"Okay." Alice stared at the mess oozing down the wall. "I'm listening."

Zoe told her what had just happened at Mill Lake Park.

"Start the car," Alice said to Harris when Zoe got to the part about leaving April behind. "But I'll drive. I know the way."

Alice pulled on her coat and stuffed Cassy into her snowsuit and herded the girls into the car.

"How the hell long has all this been going on?" Alice was driving too fast. Zoe gripped the door handle and didn't answer. "Tell me, damn it!"

"Since forever."

"Jesus, don't you be flippant with me. Not now." Alice screeched into the parking lot at Mill Lake. She yanked Cassy out of her carseat, parked her on her hip and waited for Zoe to lead the way. "Hurry up!"

"They might still be there."

"Yeah, so hurry up. If they're still there I'll kick the shit out of them myself."

The Beckoners had gone, but April was still there. She was so badly beaten that Zoe would've sworn it wasn't April huddled on the wet ground behind the bandstand. April's eyes were both swollen shut, there were several more burn marks on her face which was purple all over. April tried to speak through her split lips.

"They gone?"

"Don't move, hon." Alice knelt beside April. "Keep your head still. Where does it hurt, baby?"

"All ober."

"Harris..." Alice handed Cassy to Zoe. "You stay put and keep an eye out for those monsters."

Zoe watched her mother sprint across the park to phone an ambulance. Zoe hoped April's father wasn't working that night. Zoe squatted beside April, afraid to touch her anywhere. She looked all wrong, twisted and puffy and bloody. Cassy stretched towards her, murmuring, "owie" with the solemnity only a baby can get away with.

It wasn't April's father who came with the ambulance. It was two women, who worked silently and efficiently, loading April onto a stretcher and into the ambulance. Alice demanded to ride with her to the hospital.

"If you're not family, ma'am," the taller of the two said, "I'm afraid we can't let you do that."

Alice got right into her face and roared, "You let me ride with that little girl or I will put up such a stink you won't know what hit you!"

The shorter attendant nodded to the other and the two relented, stepping aside so Alice could climb in.

Zoe picked up April's jacket and one of her boots. On the ground beside the boot was one of Beck's eight ball matchbooks. It had one match left. Zoe lit it, letting the flame burn down to her fingertips as she headed back to the car behind Cassy and Harris.

"Those kids hassle you too?" Harris asked after several blocks of silence.

"Not anymore," Zoe said.

"They give you any more trouble, you come tell me." He glanced at her in the dark.

"You won't be here to do anything about it." Zoe didn't bother keeping her tone civil. "You live in Whitehorse, remember?"

April's parents beat Harris and Zoe to the hospital and were in with April and the doctors by the time they got there. Alice was sitting with Lewis in the waiting room. Lewis was driving one of his cars across the orange vinyl benches that lined the room.

"You can't go in there." He nodded gravely at the Emergency room's swinging doors. "I can't neither. April's broken."

"She's not broken, hon." Alice pulled him to her. "She's hurt."

"Mommy cried," Lewis reported to Zoe.

"How is she?" Zoe asked. She laid Cassy, who'd fallen asleep in the car, on a wide corner bench and covered her with her jacket.

"Bad," Alice mouthed over Lewis's head. Then she said, "Oh, she'll be just fine."

They waited for hours. Leaf joined them, after a tearful phone call from Zoe. A while later Simon and Teo arrived. They'd just come back from Christmas dinner at Simon's father's house in Vancouver and had got the frantic message from his mother. Alice took Lewis and Cassy home to bed around nine, despite Lewis's protests that Santa wouldn't know where to find him. Teo bought coffees from the vending machine, and the four of them sat, bleary-eyed, waiting.

Just after ten, Barb emerged, still wearing the snowman apron she'd had on when she'd answered the phone earlier.

"She'll be okay," she nodded. "Thank the good Lord. She'll be okay."

The four of them stared at her, waiting for more.

"She's got a lot of stitches." Barb wound and unwound an apron tie around her finger. "Too many to count. Her arm's broken. And they need to get in there to fix her knee, something with the ligaments, but that'll happen later on. She'll be fine though. Nothing that won't heal with prayer and time."

"That's great," Leaf said with a lack of conviction they all felt.

"Yeah." Simon picked at a loose thread on his shirt. "That's really great."

"Thanks be to God," Barb said. She looked at each of the four of them and then slumped into the seat beside Zoe.

"She won't say who did this to her!" She started weeping.

Zoe put a hand on Barb's shoulder and eyed the boys. They could tell, but why hadn't April? It was the perfect opportunity. The Beckoners would be charged with assault; the police would actually be able to *do* something. But did she have a reason? They owed it to her to check with her before they said anything, didn't they?

Leaf didn't think so. He eyeballed the others, mouthing, "We have to tell."

When Barb went back in to April, the four of them discussed the matter, or rather, the three of them convinced Leaf to wait until they talked to April before they told anyone. They weren't allowed to see her that night though, so Teo drove everyone home, with plans to pick them up at nine so they could see her first thing.

The hospital was very quiet Christmas morning. April was awake. She was sitting up, eating porridge, the five other beds in the room empty.

"Anything else hurts to chew," she said as a greeting.

"You okay?" Simon said.

"I guess."

"Does it hurt?" Teo asked.

"All over."

There was an awkward silence. The three of them looked at Zoe. They'd flipped a coin in the car to see who would ask her why she hadn't told about the Beckoners. Zoe had lost, but she didn't want to ask her yet. April looked too bruised to think.

Leaf eyeballed Zoe. Zoe shook her head.

"Fine," he muttered. "I'll do it. Why didn't you tell the cops who did it?"

"Beck said she'd kill me if I told."

Simon sat on the edge of the bed and took her good hand lightly in his. "You have to tell, April."

April shook her head. "No."

"You're going to let them get away with this?" Leaf started pacing. "You could be dead! They could've killed you! You want to be another Reena Virk?"

"I'm not going to tell."

There was no convincing her to tell. Teo and Simon and Leaf spent nearly an hour trying to convince her otherwise, but Zoe didn't try very hard. She didn't doubt that the Beckoners would kill her. When April's parents and Lewis showed up, arms loaded with presents, the four of them left, walking silently back to Blouise.

In the end, it was Leaf who told. He just picked up the phone, dialed the police and told them who did it. It took less than a minute. He was proud of himself, and so was Wish, who was the one who convinced him to do it with or without April's consent. Teo was happy about it; he hadn't slept well in the two days since the attack. Simon was uneasy about it. Zoe was downright terrified, as was April.

When Leaf confessed what he'd done, April shook her head. She was too mad to cry. Too scared. Too sore.

"Do you believe in God?" she asked him.

"No."

"You don't?"

"No, I don't."

April closed her eyes and laid back on the pillows. "Could you pray anyway?"

For several days there was no word from the Beckoners, no sign, no hint at retribution, which Leaf took to mean they'd been scared off for good, now that the cops were involved. April's parents insisted on pressing charges, although April tried to talk them out of it. They would not listen to her pleas to let it go.

"You're safe now, April," her father told her as they helped her out of the car the day she was released from the hospital. "It's all over."

The first time April left the house after coming home from the hospital was to go with Zoe and Leaf and Simon and Teo to Simon's house for a New Year's Eve tea party, hosted by his chic public relations mother and her slick marketing exec boyfriend, both of whom thought that Simon being gay was quaint and having him and his "little friends" there would add "panache" to the party. None of them felt particularly panache-ful that day. April was trying to give Leaf the silent treatment, but she wasn't very good at it. It was more of a cold shoulder, which Leaf understood and was gracious about, which kind of made giving him the cold shoulder pointless. Teo and Simon had had a fight before leaving, because Teo hadn't wanted to go at all.

"I feel like a gay poster boy," he said as he yanked at his tie. "I hate that your mother calls me your 'Nice Gay Boyfriend from Puerto Rico.'"

"Well, you are my nice gay boyfriend." Simon tried to sooth him before they went in.

"My family's been in this country for two generations, Simon."

Furthermore, Shadow was not allowed to come to the party. For April, the worst part about being in the hospital was being separated from Shadow. It was the first time in all her life she hadn't slept with him. When she came home, Shadow lived up to his name even more than usual. He never once left her side. When April ordered him to stay behind when they left her house on New Year's Day, no one could have guessed it would be the last time April would see him alive.

The party was barely tolerable. The five of them were on their best behavior, making polite small talk, avoiding people's indiscreet questions about April's injuries. They tugged at their fancy clothes and tried hard not to spill anything in the strictly white décor house. And then Teo "accidentally" spilled a glass of red wine—Simon's mother considered it cosmopolitan to let them drink—on the delicate lacy drapes, which is when Simon announced, in a huff, that it was time to leave. Leaf and Zoe and April glumly pulled on their coats and hurried through the rain ahead of Simon and Teo, who were stuck arguing in the middle of the driveway, oblivious to the downpour.

Barb rushed down the walk when they pulled up to April's. She wasn't wearing a jacket and she was soaked to the bone, her thin curls plastered flat against her forehead. The wide straps of her bra and the outline of her cross showed through her wet tracksuit top.

"I can't find Shadow!"

April scrambled out of the car with her crutches. "What do you mean?"

"After you left, I put him out to pee and when I opened the door to let him back in, he was gone. The gate was open. Lewis must've left it open. But he's never taken off before, not even if it was wide open. For heaven's sake, the stupid old thing is probably out looking for you."

"No, he's not. He wouldn't leave. Shadow!" April hobbled down the path, whistling for him. "Shadow, here boy!"

"We'll look in the other direction!" Simon hollered after her as Teo turned Blouise around.

They drove slowly up and down the streets around Paradise Heights, silent except for the *wush-wush* of the windshield wipers, and to take turns calling for Shadow every block or so. Shadow had vanished. Zoe asked everyone they saw if they'd seen the old black dog, but it was getting dark and there weren't many people out. Those that were were huddled behind umbrellas tilted into the icy wind; all they could see was their feet. They searched for two and a half hours, doubling back after an hour to collect April, who was shaking with cold and sobbing uncontrollably.

"It was them!" She wiped another spot in the fogged up window with her sleeve. "It was the Beckoners. I know it. Shadow wouldn't leave on his own."

"What if he saw another dog?" Leaf said.

"Or he thought he saw you?" Teo offered.

"He waits on the mat by the front door." April shook her head. "He doesn't budge until I come home. The farthest he goes without me is to the curb to watch for me after school.

That's it. Even if you dangled a steak in front of him, he wouldn't go anywhere without me."

Back at April's, Zoe called Janika's on the off chance that she could convince her to tell her if they knew anything about Shadow's disappearance. There was no answer. There was no answer at Beck's either. Heather's little brother picked up when she phoned Heather's house, but when she asked to speak to Heather, he said she wasn't there and neither was Beck or anybody, although Zoe would swear later that she heard voices in the background.

Zoe, Leaf, Simon and Teo sat on April's bed while she wept and sobbed and moaned. Simon kept apologizing for being allergic to dogs, even though nobody thought for one minute that his allergies made it his fault. Even if he weren't allergic, Shadow would never have been allowed in Simon's immaculate house anyway. Lewis sat in the doorway, apologizing for leaving the gate open, although they all knew it wasn't his fault either. Leaf offered an apology too, for telling the cops. No one argued with him on that one.

The guys grew restless, perched on the bed, knees jiggling, not sure what to do with themselves, except for Simon who rubbed April's back and told her everything was going to be fine, which probably wasn't the best idea and not at all true.

Finally, they left, mumbling long, drawn-out good-byes, lingering in the doorway with their hands in their pockets like someone had died. Zoe told them she'd call if Shadow came back, or if they heard anything from any of the posters they'd hastily put up. Zoe phoned Alice and told her she was sleeping over, and then Lewis came up to tell the girls that dinner was ready. No coaxing in the world could get April to go down, not even for a cup of hot tea. She was still wearing the clothes she'd worn all day, and they were damp and clinging to her cold skin. Zoe put a blanket over her and went downstairs to eat.

The next morning, it was Zoe who saw him first, when she got up to go pee. On the way back from the bathroom, she sleepily pulled aside the curtain, hoping to see snow. It was still raining, a bleak drizzle through the early morning haze hovering low over the roofs. Then she looked down. At first she didn't register what she was looking at, but her heart did. Her pulse quickened. She felt suddenly dizzy. Something was hanging from the apple tree. A garbage bag? A dark heavy jacket thrown over the fence? A stuffed animal?

It was Shadow, hanging from a rope around his neck, a noose, tied to the same thick branch the mannequin had been hung from. Zoe stared at him for a moment, paws limp, nose pointing to the ground, like there was something interesting there he wanted to get to and if she went out into the rain and cut him down, he'd bee-line for it, tail wagging. Zoe sank to the floor, heart racing.

April was still asleep, lying on her side, quilt pulled up under her chin, one arm clutching her pillow, knees bent out of habit, making the space Shadow had curled up in almost every night of his life, space for her best friend in the whole wide miserably unfriendly world, her best friend who was now softly swaying outside in the cold dank rain, dead.

Zoe didn't wake her. Instead, she crept down the hall and knocked softly on Barb and John's door.

"For heaven's sake, Lewis." Barb's voice was gravelly with sleep. "It's not locked."

Zoe hesitated, and then opened the door.

"Oh, Zoe. What's wrong?" Barb lumbered off the bed and into her robe. "Are you sick? Is it April?"

Zoe stood in the doorway, stunned silent, drinking in the stale perfume of the room: Barb's apple soap, John's spicy cologne that before had seemed so cloying but now was an elixir. She wanted to shut the door and lock the three of them in and never leave that place. She wanted to crawl between them, go to sleep, and wake up five years old with these plain, solid, faithful people as her parents. People who make their kids eat whole wheat bread and carrot sticks, parents who limit how much TV their kids watch. Parents who'd get their lonely misfit kid a dog in the first place. Parents who'd let that dog sleep with the kid, even if he did shed all over, even if he did start to stink something awful as he got old.

"It's Shadow," Zoe said. "You better come."

Zoe led Barb downstairs. The two of them stood at the patio door, gazing through the rain at the dog. Barb clutched her cross and cried. Zoe stood there, shivering, until Barb caught her breath and managed to speak.

"I don't want her to see." Zoe almost sighed with relief at Barb's firm decisive tone. "We won't say a word. Not even to John. They can think he ran away, or got hit by a car. Sweet Jesus, anything but this."

Wordlessly, Zoe followed Barb as she collected shears, a step stool, and a big blue tarp to wrap him in. They'd just stepped out into the rain, both of them in yellow ambulance-issue slickers, when they heard April. They looked up. April was standing, or had just been standing, at her window. Her scream shook the suspended morning, its heartrending force pushing the fog towards the mountains, the rain back up the valley, the clouds back to sea. By the time they got upstairs, by the time Barb sank to the floor and took April in her arms, the sky was a cloudless blue, the cold winter sun peeking over the snow-capped mountains of a brand new year.

the plan

Leaf came over to help John take Shadow down. Barb was still upstairs with April, Lewis had been hurriedly steered out the front door to the neighbors, still in his pajamas, his father's large hands acting as blinders, but still, they whispered. Who would cut the rope? Who would hold his weight? Where they would put him once they got him down?

First though, John called the police. He walked ever so slowly to the phone, like it was ten miles away rather than ten steps. He spoke softly, calmly to the police, and then he went upstairs to pray with Barb and April until the cops arrived. He'd invited Leaf and Zoe to join them, but Leaf had shook his head for the both of them. They sat huddled on the couch, backs to the window. In the quiet, Zoe could hear John's deep voice intoning upstairs in April's room, pleading with God. Every once in a while Barb's voice would join in for an "Amen," or "Sweet Jesus."

"They want a miracle?" Leaf glanced up at the ceiling again. "It's a miracle she hasn't killed herself already, with everything those assholes put her through."

When Leaf said that, Zoe's mind cleared for a sharp, focused second, and then the idea came, complete and brilliant.

"You're absolutely right." She lifted his arm off her shoulder and sat up. "It's perfect."

"What?"

"She did."

"Did what?"

"She *did* kill herself."

"What are you talking about, Zoe?"

"Listen," she grabbed his knee. "Listen to me. After she found Shadow this morning, she hung herself, and she left a note naming the Beckoners, *blaming* the Beckoners." Zoe stood up and began to pace. "Those girls in Mission were *charged* after that happened there last year. It's brilliant!"

Upstairs the praying was getting louder. John was on his feet, pacing in time with his prayer, his step extra heavy whenever he called out, "Jesus!" And then, all of a sudden, April was at the foot of the stairs. Leaf scrambled over the back of the couch and yanked the curtains shut. Until that moment, it had seemed inappropriate to close them, like they'd be shutting Shadow out, as if he'd done something wrong.

"My dad's on a roll." April pointed to the chandelier shuddering over the dining room table. "He started out praying for me, and for Shadow. But now he's praying for the Beckoners. I couldn't stand it." She sat on the bottom step, her good hand held tight between her knees.

"We have an idea." Zoe sat beside her and explained it all.

"You don't have to go along with it," Leaf said after Zoe was finished and April still hadn't said anything. "I'm not so sure it's a good idea."

After another long silence, April got up. She opened the curtains and looked straight at Shadow. "I'll do it."

The police arriving was the first part. Zoe watched out of Lewis's window. Sure enough, across the lane and down six doors, Janika's bedroom curtains were open and more than one face was watching. Zoe squinted. Heather, Beck and Janika. Maybe the others were there too, but maybe not, and it didn't matter. The plan would work even if it was only Janika who saw, though Zoe didn't doubt that all the Beckoners were at Janika's that morning to watch the fallout. Zoe watched the girls watch the police arrive. She'd read somewhere once that serial killers start out by hurting animals. Did they know that? Which one of them actually did it, she wondered. Brady? Beck? Had they been stoned? Drunk? High on the hype of each other?

Downstairs, John was dealing with the police. Two cars had come, which only added to the plan but happened only because it was a slow New Year's Day so far for the cops. All four officers had been at the truck stop out by the highway. When they'd heard it was only a dead dog, they'd taken their time, which had been just enough time to convince Barb and John to go along with Zoe's plan.

One set of cops took pictures while the other took notes and questioned John on the front step. John answered each question, and if any of the cops thought he was overly upset over a dead dog, none of them acted like it. John was already acting, even though he wouldn't have to really start until after the police left.

April's dad had not been easily sold on the idea, but then April told him about the mannequin and then told him it was the only thing that would make the Beckoners stop forever. He'd agreed to go along with it, after taking a few minutes to pray in private about it with Barb upstairs.

Jesus must've agreed. They came down, holding hands, agreeing to the plan as though God himself had whispered in their ears that if they didn't go along with this their precious lamb of His might just go ahead and kill herself for real, or run away and become a crack-addicted whore dying on the streets of Vancouver.

Teo and Simon came over, slipping in through the back. John looked sidelong and critically at them as they climbed the stairs to Lewis's room. Simon and Zoe kept track of what was happening at Janika's window the whole time. While the police were still there, an ambulance pulled up, lights flashing, sirens soberly quiet. Right on time and doing the trick beautifully. The Beckoners were all at the window now, even Brady and Trevor, all crammed together, staring out. Zoe looked through Lewis's binoculars. April came up to look, and so did Leaf, taking turns peeking through the heavy curtains.

"They're shoving past each other to get a better view!" Leaf laughed.

April didn't laugh. She took the binoculars and watched the Beckoners panic.

When the police left, Zoe went downstairs and joined the others at the table while Barb maniacally served up pancakes. Barb and April and Zoe couldn't eat, but John and Leaf and John's two colleagues, who were actually on call and said they'd be glad to help so long as they weren't called out in the meantime, ate more than their fair share. Simon and Teo stayed upstairs. They said they didn't mind keeping watch. They said they weren't hungry, but Zoe knew it was because of April's parent's disapproval of them.

One of the ambulance attendants had a ponytail and a tribal tattoo circling his left biceps. That was McEwen. He loved the plan. Doug, the driver, was much older and rather quiet about the whole idea. His jaw clicked when he chewed.

"All right then." John emptied his coffee mug in one swallow. "Let's get this over with."

"Yeah, okay," McEwen shoveled another fork full of pancake into his mouth, downed a glass of orange juice and pushed back his chair. "I'll get the stretcher."

Doug kept eating, chewing slowly. "Holler when you need me," he said between clicks.

"Think of it as a movie and we're all the actors," Zoe said. "Doug, all you have to do is drive. Barb and John will do the hard work."

"They're going nuts!" Simon called from upstairs. "They're coming outside!"

It was working beautifully.

McEwen was back, a proud grin on his face. "I made sure those little tweakers saw me unroll the body bag."

John rooted through the storage closet, looking for Annie, the full-sized CPR doll he used when he taught First Aid in the church basement. He yanked her free from the tangle of beach gear and with the help of McEwen zipped her into the black body bag.

It was a creepy thing to see, that full body bag—the outline of Annie, head to toe. It was very convincing.

"Givin' me the willies," McEwen said.

Zoe watched Barb and John. They were holding hands, eyes closed, praying again. For what? Annie? April? The Beckoners?

"Get it out of here," April said, turning away.

"Sure, sweetheart." McEwen nodded at Doug, who reluctantly put down his fork and wiped his mouth before helping to lift Annie onto the stretcher. As they made their way to the door, Zoe, April and Leaf raced upstairs to join Simon and Teo to watch what the Beckoners would do when they laid eyes on the full body bag being lifted into the ambulance.

The Beckoners were all outside now, as were most of the neighbors too. Barb had worried that might happen, but Zoe was glad, it only made the charade so much more believable, and Barb could go around later and explain it was just John and his buddies playing a prank.

The Beckoners turned to each other as McEwen and Doug lifted the stretcher into the back of the ambulance. Janika's hands covered her mouth. Jazz stared, arms limp at her sides. Lindsay and Heather argued loudly. Brady and Trevor stood far apart, hands in their pockets, not looking at anybody or each other. Beck sat on the step, head in her hands.

John and Barb wept for real. Zoe didn't have to wonder where they summoned the tears from. All it would've taken would be to imagine if it really was April in that body bag. John put his arm around Barb's shoulders and held her close while McEwen shut the doors and Doug started the engine. Then, as the ambulance drove away, his knees buckled and he fell to the ground, overcome with grief. But it wasn't really grief. The black humor of it had suddenly hit him. He was covering his face so the Beckoners wouldn't see him laughing uncontrollably. Barb helped him up, and then the two of them came inside, leaning heavily on each other.

April handed the binoculars to Zoe. "Now what?"

"Now we wait." Zoe watched the Beckoners file back inside, shoulders slumped, faces drenched in shock. It had worked. They thought April had killed herself because of them.

panic

The Beckoners had no one else to turn to except Zoe. When Zoe got home, after she'd set April up with an armload of videos and a bag of junk food, the curtains pinned shut, there were ten messages from Janika, all begging her to call. Zoe took a deep breath and dialed.

"What happened?" Janika was frantic. "What's going on?"

"Like you don't know." Zoe's voice was steel.

"Oh, God. She didn't. Oh my God." Janika pulled away from the phone. "She did!" She screamed at the others. "She killed herself!"

Zoe waited quietly.

"What are we going to do?" Janika screamed down the phone. In the background, Heather and Lindsay yelled at each other.

"It's your fault!" Lindsay screamed.

"It wasn't even me!" Heather screeched, her voice tight with fear. "It's Brady's fault! If he never hit the dog none of this would be happening."

"Yeah?" Brady's voice wavered dangerously close to tears. "Who told me to head straight for it, huh? Don't play all innocent, Heather. You're just as covered in shit as the rest of us."

"Janika?" Zoe said her name softly.

"Shut up! Everybody just shut the fuck up!" Janika's voice shook. "Yeah?"

"She left a note, Janika."

"I have to go."

"There was a note, with your names…"

"I never meant—" Janika's voice caught. "We didn't mean—"

"Mean what?" Zoe tried not to sound icy.

Janika couldn't talk. She just cried and cried while Zoe happily listened to the Beckoners rip each other apart in the background.

"I can't deal with this," Janika finally choked out before hanging up the phone.

Zoe set the phone down. Janika would call back. They would want to know what the note said.

When Janika called back late that night, Zoe made sure she spoke clearly and calmly.

"It would be best if you all went to the police."

"We can't do that!" Janika said in between sobs. "We already got assault charges!"

"You have to. The note blames all of you. By name." Zoe had written down what she wanted to say, just in case she got swept up in Janika's very real fear and blurted out the truth. She was almost tempted, hearing how upset Janika was, but she kept to the script.

"If you don't go, they'll come for you." Zoe touched the words with her finger as she said them. "That would be worse. You want them breaking down your doors and cuffing you in front of your parents? Wouldn't it be better if you all went and explained yourselves as best as you could? It would look better for all of you, especially after what happened in the park." There was a long pause.

"You think so?" Janika blew her nose.

"Yes."

"We have to tell our parents?"

"First, yes," Zoe said. "And then the cops. Tell them about the mannequin, and Shadow, and April. There's no other way."

"You think the others will agree?"

"You have to do it together, Janika. You're all in it together." That was the last thing Zoe had written to say. She wanted to hang up the phone before she said anything more, anything that might make Janika suspicious. "I'm sorry that you—" Zoe stopped herself. "Look, the sooner you do it, the sooner it'll be over with."

There was a long silence. Janika had stopped crying.

"Janika, are you there?"

"I'm here," Janika whispered. "We'll go tomorrow."

snow

Simon knew of a café across the street from the police station that would be perfect to watch from. The Coffee Snob was still decorated for the holidays, sort of. The entrance was strung with lights, but red ones in the shape of chili peppers, green ones like cacti and yellow ones like cowboy hats. There was a tree, but it was a solstice tree, a sign on it said so, and it was decorated with anarchist symbols and peace signs twisted out of pipe cleaners, and little anti-Christmas manifestos written by various patrons on construction paper. The sole barista was curled up in an easy chair by an electric heater under a wall plastered with posters advertising political rallies and literary readings. He was reading Proust, which he reluctantly put down after Zoe, Leaf, Simon, Teo and April had been waiting at the counter for ages, eyes on the door to the kitchen, expecting someone to come from there. He rolled his eyes at the other customers, who all looked like they were doing downtime between anti-globalization protests.

"Help yourself next time you come, okay?" He made their coffees, walking them through how the espresso machine worked, and then he showed them how to work the till, which had a sticker on it that read, Karma kills short-changers.

There were no tables available by the window. At one, an elderly couple dressed in brown cords and matching thick wool sweaters played chess. At the other, a student was sluggishly highlighting an enormous college textbook.

"Excuse me, sir? Ma'am?" Simon approached the elderly couple after the student scowled at him when he got within five feet of her table. "We're conducting a bit of a stake-out here, and we need to keep our eyes on the police station. Do you think—" before he could explain further, the couple pushed their chairs back and stood.

"Anything to keep thumbs on the pigs, son." The man winked behind his wire-rimmed glasses, carefully lifting the board so the pieces wouldn't slide. "We'll sit over there."

After two rounds of coffee the five of them were buzzing, barely able to sit still. They took turns watching for the Beckoners. Except for Simon, who could not sit still at all. He was making the rounds, dazzling the customers with his slick wit, sidling up to them with a smooth, "So what brings you here?" Soon, he had everyone gathered around their table, which they'd pushed together with the college student's, who'd finally given up studying. Simon had everyone engulfed in a rowdy game of Go Fish using two decks the barista produced, one with Fidel Castro on the back, the other with nude fifties pin-up models. Even April was laughing, cheeks flushed, probably from all the caffeine and the space heater beside the table. When she smiled her eyes pinched up a little and she tilted her head to the side in a way that was almost cute.

The barista, Zoe was astonished to see, was definitely checking April out. Zoe wouldn't have believed it if she hadn't seen it with her own eyes, but when he came back with yet another tray of lattes, Tim hovered until Teo got up to pee, and then he swooped in and took Teo's chair, which just happened to be the one beside April. In between his turns, Tim leaned on his elbows and took off his glasses and asked her questions, which she answered easily. It was as if that café, that humid, low-ceilinged stuffy room was a chrysalis, and April was transforming into a new version of herself right before Zoe's eyes.

"Is that them?" Tim nodded at the window.

Zoe and the others rushed to the glass, their breath fogging it up. They wiped it clear and watched. Five cars. All the Beckoners, all at once, which was better than Zoe could've hoped for, complete with various attending adults, all with the same moist-eyed fury and shoulder-slumping disappointment.

Beck climbed out of the backseat of her parents' car and stood on the sidewalk alone for a moment while the others were ushered into the station, parents gripping their children's elbows. Beck watched her friends go ahead of her. April and Zoe watched Beck, noses to the glass like little kids watching the first snow fall. The others had stepped away and were talking behind them, voices hushed, as though Beck might hear all the way across the street, through the brick walls and thick glass.

In his travels around the café, Simon had told the story to everyone, and now they were united in rage and sympathy and angst, each of them reciting their own bullied histories with comraderie they'd normally reserve for protest highlights: paddy wagon moments, the first time they got hauled off to jail, bodies civil-disobediently limp, arms linked for peace.

Beck's mother finally got out of the car. A small woman with an angular face, she stood on the sidewalk, clutching her purse strap tight with both hands. She stared at Beck's back.

Beck's father leaned across the interior of the car and rolled the passenger window down to say something to her mother. Beck's mother looked away from her husband and Beck, down the sidewalk in the other direction, shaking her head at whatever he was saying. He raised his voice, craning his neck out the window to address Beck, who did not turn to receive his words. He hauled himself back in front of the wheel and took off, tires slashing through puddles.

Beck stood still as her mother passed her, chin up, still clutching her purse, hugging the side of the building like she didn't want to get too close to her daughter. Then Beck was alone, eyes on the ground. She looked naked despite her down jacket, her scarf, her clunky winter boots, like she was a paper doll underneath: flat, flimsy, easily stripped.

That night Harris and Leaf built a bonfire on the beach at Mill Lake. Alice brought a bag of turkey sandwiches. Wish brought thermoses of hot chocolate. Simon and Teo brought marshmallows and slabs of chocolate and graham wafers to make s'mores. Tim brought cherry and almond biscotti. Zoe brought colored markers for everyone to sign April's cast, which no one had thought to do yet. April brought Shadow's ashes in a small cardboard box.

Barb and John did not believe that animals had souls, or could go to heaven, but they had agreed to pay for the cremation anyway. When the fire was down to embers, and Cassy and Connor were asleep on Harris's and Wish's laps, and Lewis had to fight to keep his eyes open, April hobbled to the water and let Shadow's ashes scatter in the night. Zoe had brought one other thing from home—her travelling star. She shone a flashlight on it for a couple of minutes, and then walked with the boys down to the water. She threw the travelling star into the trail of ashes, where it floated and glowed, a bright star slipping away on the black water, as a gentle snow began to fall.